EVIL IS SHE...

L.L. WACKENS

BALBOA.PRESS
A DIVISION OF HAY HOUSE

Balboa Press books may be ordered through booksellers or by contacting:

Balboa Press
A Division of Hay House
1663 Liberty Drive
Bloomington, IN 47403
www.balboapress.com
844-682-1282

ISBN: 978-1-9822-5212-0 (sc)
ISBN: 978-1-9822-5213-7 (e)

Balboa Press rev. date: 08/11/2020

This book is dedicated to my son Kasim…
If I can do it, you can as well son.

ACKNOWLEDGEMENT

First and foremost I want to thank ALLAH(swt),if not for his mercy there would be book.

Next, all those that helped in the tasks that brought this book to life, Travona Herrington, keep them ventures up, yellowbagg, health smoothies and the online hip hop magazine, Zabrina ann Jobe for the long nights of typing you offered, Janice, Fatty, Shy, for the proof reading y'all done for me. My niece Tamoo for helping with converting and paperwork.

And to all my men that's out the way but trying to see better days keep shining I'm a try my best to walk the walk for as long as my feet will last.

CONTENTS

PART III AN EMPIRE CRUMBLED

PART ONE

HOME SWEET HOME

1.1 HOME AGAIN

6 a.m. the sound of reveille roars though the cell block. Echoing like the hollowness of the Grand Canyon. To some this sound only symbolized the start of a new beginning.

To others it's just a continuance from the chaos once set loose throughout the cities, towns, boroughs and counties in which their terror had harvested.

The echoing of such a sound only awakens the lions, lambs and wolves from the caves in which they dwell.

For many this sound is dreaded. It only means the terror starts all over again. A second chance to wish for death.

For Mujahid, this sound only meant he was within hours of becoming a productive part of society. Or on his last leg on a journey to a land where only his kind and people of his kind could lay foundation in order to wreak havoc.

This was his 1825th day of a sentence he thought would never end.

Upon receiving this sentence, he was a young wild renegade without any sense of direction.

Entering the tunnel of what he thought would be the eternal light, he consumed the overall attitude that only the strong survive.

Who would of ever thought Mujahid of all people would see the light of day ever again after all the havoc he reeked.

Somehow his sentencing judge felt that because of his age it was still hope for his soul to rectify his evil ways.

1

Little did he realize Mujahid had been without a soul since the tender age of nine. This had been the ripe and tender age when the streets took his father's life. And replaced the values that he tried to instill in Mujahid with the reality that the streets don't love no one.

"Mr. Abdus-Samad report to the bridge" was the sound that alerted Mujahid and the rest of the housing unit that it was time to exit the den and begin a journey into new lands with an old face.

On his way to the bridge Mujahid felt like he had just begun to walk the longest mile of his already wretched life.

The cell block he had been housed on was D block, better known as, The Terror Dome. In the most notorious penitentiary in Pennsylvania, S.C.I. Graterford.

D block's housing unit was as long as two city blocks, four hundred cells, two tiers high housing six hundred men.

Within the institution there was five cell blocks, A through E, on what the inmates referred to as the old side.

This is where it went down, a city within a city. Any and everything a person could and would want, including the extras that accompanies the treasures of pussy was available for the right price.

There was more narcotics within the confines of the institution then on the streets of Philadelphia.

Bosses of bosses, playas, hustlers, street pharmacists, murderers, rapist, pedophiles, weirdos and every other lifestyle imaginable to a man occupied this institution. therefore, on a daily basis the hustle got greater.

Real niggas knew that guns got checked in at the gate. Therefore, if you weren't who you proclaimed to be, a nigga was definitely gone expose the true nature of your so called character. The first sign of fear only meant the wolves was coming.

Even if you were scared, you better not allow it to prevail. It was more beneficial to just let the fear stay locked up inside and just echo into the emptiness of your soul. The mere sight of weakness was surely enough to have a mister become a misses.

Mujahid had seen the best of the so called goons and thugs choose panties over steel.

Once Mujahid had reached the bridge, the nut ass C.O. told him,"

It was time for discharge."

He grabbed his pass to the receiving room and without looking back he exited the block. All who didn't know or seen him leaving wouldn't see him.

Mujahid never understood how, or why, men took so much time to leave the hell hole they dwelled in, for many the majority of their lives, when it was time to go.

Later on Mujahid learned that to many this was all they had, after living with a muthafucka for so long, so many years out of your life, you become like family. So for many this was a hard walk to take.

For Mujahid, he couldn't adjust to the train of thought or conditioning it took to comprehend to such an emotion. When it was over, it was over! No Rap! Get at me when... or if you touch was his sentiments.

Upon arrival at the receiving room Mujahid was greeted by a long haired white woman who issued him paperwork to sign. Once he surrendered his John Hancock, a check for twenty-five hundred dollars was issued to him along with two hundred in cash.

He got dressed in clothes sent up to him by his family, a pair of Nike Vapormax 360, a pair of Lenny Austin jeans, Hannyiah's fashion Polo shirt and leather, white beater and Kangol.

Once dressed an officer escorted him out of the institution to a ran down barn, which he found out was a bus station for the residents of the sticks in which he had resided. He had a nice long ride ahead of him.

After a forty-five minute wait in this raggedy bus station in the sticks, his bus finally arrived. Despite feeling way out of his element he boarded it. It kind of felt strange to be intermingling with civilians, Mujahid thought to himself.

He felt like everyone was staring at him. No doubt they knew he was a recent resident of the prison that made the economy of that poor community boom. He had been the only black man in a rural area predominantly white. He didn't really give a fuck. He sat by a window in the rear of the bus.

It's funny that Rosa Parks fought so hard to have equality and the right to sit at the front of the bus, yet, in the ghettos throughout the world, the back of the bus are the most sought after seats, Mujahid thought to himself.

A nigga would rather stand and be miserable than sit in the front of the bus.

Three and a half hours later he finally arrived in the city of Brotherly Love, Philadelphia. To him it felt good to be home. Almost as good as getting that first shot of pussy and a home cooked meal. Mujahid exited the bus and just stood in awe, amazed at how different shit looked. Almost like he was lost somewhere in time. Nevertheless, he was home.

After taking in the new sights of the city, Mujahid went to the one place he could find comfort, his hood.

A section of North Philly known as Beirut,12th and Huntingdon. This is where it all went down.

The name Beirut had been appropriate since it was literally a war zone. There wasn't a night the entire 22nd and 23rd precinct didn't have to make an appearance to calm the violence that little radius of the city had to offer.

Although it was tiny in radius, it was truly a hood of honor and glory. In most hoods it's always a name that stands out amongst the rest, but here, one name couldn't hold the weight of the hood, everybody wore their hearts on their sleeves. And for those who didn't, they weren't permitted to roam freely here.

The universal code of the streets was enforced heavily, snitches ended up in ditches, money got grabbed, bitches was bagged and rats got tagged.

In order to make an appearance on the strip you had to be somebody. And not just a boss of a boss. Your work had to be recognized throughout the city. And even then, one still had to be tested to see their makeup. What's a gun to one ain't to all, regardless of who their affiliated with.

Everybody was solo. And slayed each other on a daily basis within their own community. But when outsiders came through, they became thicker than thieves. That's when they all came together like Voltron.

It was a scary and crazy place to live, but Mujahid enjoyed the comforts of being surrounded by real niggas.

As Mujahid made his grand entrance into Beirut, he was greeted with an abundance of love by the older bunch who had known him. And as expected when an O.G. makes an appearance, the checks was broken off. Niggas was handing him money in stacks. Even the up and coming G's was breaking him off. They didn't know him, but his work was recognized and respected throughout the generations. He was basically like an urban legend, that one dude who put in so much work, that it was gone take the next G.O.rilla to fill his shoes, a lifetime to add up to his status. He was a certified five star general.

Besides the niggas, the bitches were showing love as well. They were looking to be his first shot of pussy. He had offers for threesomes, foursomes and more. These bitches were choosing, but Mujahid wasn't looking to be chose.

Even though he could have had his pick of the litter, he knew these bitches was looking to get a free ride. His name alone was gone generate paper, so for any one of them to be able to claim him was a dream come true for them. And a nightmare for Mujahid.

The woman of this era wasn't about nothing, no sense of loyalty, dedication or commitment. All they wanted was a wet ass, the chance to ride in a hot car, some weave and minutes on their phone. Regardless, of the price they had to pay to indulge. Even if it meant dishonesty, betrayal and disrespect. They just wanted to be a part of something.

Mujahid had better things in the makings. He had matured to the point all the dumb shit wasn't going down, unless necessary. He been on both sides of the fence, so he knew what was at the end of the road for a failed attempt. He gave up too much already, now was the time to focus on rebuilding what he lost and destroyed, the relationship with himself.

He had to try to put his life back in order. And a task he had in front of him. Nevertheless, he was focused and prepared to do what he had to in order for it to work, even if it meant becoming a nine to five ass nigga, he was on board.

He managed to collect enough bread to hold him down for a little while. At least until he got on his feet. For the moment, he just wanted to enjoy being free.

12. THE CONNECT

Mujahid had been home for a little over six months. According to the standards of the game, he was doing bad. But according to the standards of society, he was living a productive life.

To those who knew and loved him, they had mixed emotions. Many wanted to see him come straight home and get it, regardless of the cost. They knew if he ate his plate would hold extremely large amounts of cash, which meant their portions would be plentiful. However, to those who's hearts supported, loved and cherished every stolen moment they shared with Mujahid only wanted the humbleness to continue. Regardless of the gain involved.

As opposed too many people fresh out the penal system, Mujahid had come straight into a relationship, not giving himself time to flourish and explore his options to be certain that the life he's living is that of his choice.

All through his bid Mujahid hadn't kept in touch with nobody except this one particular lady friend who absolutely adored him. Her every wish was to become his better and other half. A high yellow, chunky, but oh so pretty, highly intelligent when it came to book smarts, but a square, L7, pointy on all corners when it came to the street life, by the name of Aisha.

In no way did she suffer from the big girl syndrome. Aisha was a sarcastic, conceited young lady, with all the confidence possible for one person to possess for themselves.

Although, in age she was just an unripened tender twenty-three, her soul warranted all the years of a forty year old woman.

Considering her background, she had come a long way and seen a lot in her youthful days. However, she became a statistic, a teenage mother at sixteen. Yet, instead of allowing her mistakes to hinder her from being all she could be, Aisha instead used them as fuel, and as inspiration, to be who and what she was destined to be. She had a son by the name of Nasir.

A typical six year old. A real smooth young boy who in his eyes, was a man.

Since Aisha had always tried to instill the values of being such into him since birth, in his eyes he was his mother's protector. As well as king of their castle. His attitude towards Mujahid was nonchalant due to the fact he had known who Mujahid was.

Mujahid had two brothers. One by the name of J.A.P.A.N, which stood for just another pimp ass nigga, who went to prison and later transformed into Hafiz. Also there was the youngest of the two, named Raheem, who had been messing with Aisha's younger sister Amirah, who at this point had a child by Raheem. A pretty little girl by the name of Zandria.

After Mujahid's first bid he met Aisha. She was a young girl with a sassy attitude. But somehow struck the curiosity of Mujahid. He used to flat out stalk this little bitch. Determined to get at her and string her along. Only because at that time she truly believed she wasn't able to be turned out.

To Mujahid this was a challenge. And just as all things in his life, he was always willing to accept the task.

On a constant basis he pursued Aisha for two years. Until finally Christmas eve of 2018. That's when she invited Mujahid over her apartment to help clean and prepare to entertain her guest the following day. What started out as work, soon ended up as an everlasting fuck fest. And from that point on Mujahid and Aisha was homies with benefits.

She had her life as did he. But every now and then they would meet in the middle to enjoy the moment.

As the days turned into weeks and weeks into months their bond grew. Not knowing how neither one felt towards the other, Mujahid was arrested. And throughout his stay in the correctional system, all he had was Aisha.

Eventually they explored, journeyed and conquered the task of getting to know one another. Before long, they had become an item.

Being who he was, Mujahid felt it was only right to come home and explore the possibilities of being with Aisha.

Being together the last six months had been challenging for Mujahid. He was a person of the streets with the soul of the game. So eventually the temptations had outweighed the yearning for the life he was living.

One day, a Monday to be exact, Mujahid receives a phone call.

"Hello" he said.

On the other end of the receiver came a soft spoken heavy down south accented voice uttering the words, "What's up partner!"

"Who this?" Mujahid asked in a tone that showed his curiosity.

"It's Tone." He replied in a happy tone like they were being reunited after years of separation.

"Tone who?" Mujahid said with confusion expressed on his face and voice.

Then that same voice spoke these words, "We walked for all those years around the yard... You was my brother behind that wall... Now you don't know me."

"Oh shit!... Damn!... My bad Pretty Tone, damn when you touch?"

Mujahid asked.

"I been home for a month and a half." Tone replied.

"So what's poppin' out Pittsburgh?"

"I ain't in the burg... I'm in Philly. Just like I told you, once I touch, you on!

And as a man I'm honoring my word. So when can I get with you?

I plan on being in Philly for at least five days. I want to meet and talk to you." said Tone.

"Well, let me get a shower and I'm a hit you back soon as I'm done," Mujahid replied.

"Don't you need the number?" Tone asked.

"Naw! I got caller I.D. the number pops up automatically, so just let me take care of my hygiene and I'm a get at you A.S.A.P." Mujahid said.

"Bet!" was all Tone said before hanging up.

Smiling like a Cheshire cat, Mujahid couldn't believe Tone was really who he had always professed to be. Inside the penitentiary he was a quiet soft spoken kind of cat. He was always humble. But when he talked, he spoke like he was crazy!... or at least the contents of his speech sounded crazy to Mujahid.

One thing you learn in jail is everybody can be whoever they wanted to be. So naturally when Tone spoke of transporting hundreds of kilos of cocaine and heroin to all these crazy destinations, Mujahid just shrugged it off as bullshit. If he wanted to be a kingpin, or drug lord in his world, he was entitled to be that. It's his story to be told as he chooses.

Never once really entertaining the thought that Tone was, or could be, who he always expressed to be to Mujahid he really was. Pausing and showing signs of deep thought meditation, Mujahid was now baffled as to what Tone wanted with him.

Still unwilling to believe that this man could actually be the black Pablo Escobar he so many times referred to himself as.

Now curious to meet and greet Tone, Mujahid had gone through his normal routine in preparing to transform into EL.

EL was his alter ego. The G.O.rilla who the streets had come to respect.

In a matter of an hour and a half Mujahid had completely descended back to that vicious nigga who the streets feared, but was respected by all and loved by few.

EL, the lunatic renegade who believed bloodshed was just a normal occurrence in the day and the life of a go getter. If it was there, he wanted it, at any cost. His motto was, if you couldn't hold it down, you shouldn't have it. This referred to everything imaginable, from the million dollar blocks, to the lint stuck in the corners of a person's pocket.

Now prepared to entertain his old jail house buddy, Mujahid made that call back to Tone.

After four rings Tone answers, "Talk to me!" Immediately identifying the number as Mujahid's.

Anticipating his immediate reply back, Mujahid spews back," Where you at?"

Tone gave him a destination that later he found out to be the Bellevue Stratton. One of the most prestigious hotels in Philadelphia. He told Mujahid to ask for Anthony Austin at the front desk.

"I'm on my way," was the response Mujahid surrendered. Completely forgetting he had a prior engagement with Aisha.

Mujahid left for the destination given to him by Tone.

Twenty minutes later, in a yellow city cab, Mujahid arrives. And as relayed to him, asks for Anthony Austin at the front desk.

The concierge picked up a red phone and dialed a four digit number. Mujahid thinking to himself, that must be his room number.

Standing there taking in the sights, Mujahid suddenly realized that after spending his whole life in this city he had never been in this hotel before. So he was taken aback by the sights. Entertaining the thought that nothing but major paper up in this bitch. Nothing but Celebrities, Politicians and prominent families who visit his lovely city of brotherly love.

Just as Mujahid slipped away that fast in a day dream of robbing this establishment, the concierge spoke to him bringing him out his daze, "Excuse me sir... room 1406. Take the last elevator to your left."

Not understanding why he had to use a particular elevator, until he had gotten on the elevator, floors 1–13 had been erased from the console. All that remained was 14–36 with initials PH for penthouse that you needed a key to access.

He arrived at the 14th floor, exited the elevator and began to walk to a sign on the wall that read 1400–1430 with an arrow that pointed to his right.

Mujahid began to walk until finally he sees 1406. He knocks on the door. A slender man wearing a custom made suit answers and greets him with an upward nod and a few choice words, "What's up!"

"Where Tone?" Mujahid replied.

He escorted Mujahid to the balcony which overlooked a small section of Center City.

They're waiting. Mujahid finally sees Tone.

"Pretty Tone!" He yelled in a playful toned voice. "What's the business?" he asked as he embraced Tone.

Tone just held out his hand as to gesture a stop motion. "Be easy, we gone get to all that... but first have a drink," offering a glass of cognac.

Mujahid accepts the drink. And more so nurses it then actually drank it. He had it in his mind that he wanted to be in a well aware and fully conscious state to discuss business. If in fact, it was the business he thought it would be.

"Since day one of meeting you, I felt you had a good sense of business and was the man I was destined to meet in order to tap into this Philly market.

Just as I told you, I'm here to cash in on my words I promised you... All those dreams you had in the box could be in the makings of becoming reality, if you choose wisely.

As for myself, I've long left the urge to dream. I set horizons, and let them become endless, cause my reality is many peoples fantasies.

The time has come for you to brush elbows with the elite. All those talks we had, I took heed. And now it's time to execute the chats." Tone said in a serious but heart felt tone.

Stuck in a semi-dazed state, in a cross of thinking this shit is not real, Mujahid asks, "What's the plan?"

"There is no plan young blood. The task is to get rid of as much material as the city can stand. You say it, it's there."

This statement had been music to Mujahid ears.

"First things first, I deal with you and only you. I don't want to meet none of your players. Secondly, our business is just that!... Our business! It's never to be spoken over phones, Third party or within the realms of the public. I call you... tell you I'll call back, automatically you know I'm on my way to get what you got available at that moment. Once I call, you come here just as you did today, ask for the same name as today.

Lastly, as men we must make an oath to one another that clearly defines who we are. And our words are respected as who we are. All the shiesty shit is not in the plans. So as a man.... My man, do you agree to the terms laid out for you?" Tone asked with a look in his eyes that let on he meant business. And nothing but business.

"Of course." Mujahid immediately replies.

"NO! NO! NO!" Tone said before briefly pausing.

Then goes on to add, "...Give me your word as a man."

"I give you my word as a man that I am who I professed to be, as well as who stands before you today." Mujahid stated with a tone that had conviction all through it.

Tone embraced Mujahid then took a drink.

"Now to the business! I got one hundred kilos of cocaine for you at 15.5 grand a block." Tone said.

"Whoooa family! That's out my range right now. Why can't we start small with a few? And as we increase clientele we get heavier?" Mujahid asked in a tone that made it perfectly clear he wasn't in that league to accept that amount yet.

"There you go putting restrictions and boundaries on yourself again. If you gone get it, then get it! You can't buy caddies making roller skate money. You'll have plenty of time to get rid of it. Especially now, cause a drought is due to hit in the next two months." Tone assured Mujahid.

Still leery and feeling pressured, Mujahid agrees to take the package, along with the duffle bag that read Smithson Cleaning Service. There was also a phone with one number programmed into it. There were dollar signs next to the number, no name.

Now at home, Mujahid walks through the door only to be greeted with an attitude by Aisha.

Totally forgetting about their plans for their evening of romance that was supposed to had started with Mujahid picking her up from work. Aisha caught Mujahid off guard with a sarcastic comment.

"I guess I needed to take a tour of this sorry ass city on the bus!" Then she proceeded to ask, "What happened to you picking me up from work?"

"I forgot baby... I apologize!... Something came up that was too important to let slide." Mujahid explained to her.

Not wanting to hear it, she stormed up the steps to prepare for their night out.

While she was doing that, Mujahid took the bag he came into the house with to the basement. He tucked it away into an old boiler that was broken. Now proceeding with the plans already prearranged. Mujahid exits the basement and heads for the bedroom to help Aisha get over her anger.

Grabbing her from behind and gently kissing on her neck, Mujahid began to say, "You know you my baby!... I'm sorry baby!... I had an unexpected visitor from out of town baby."

"And you couldn't call to say this?" Aisha asked still mad, but not as mad as initially.

"It slipped my mind, but that's over with... It's all about you baby! So what you wanna do?"

"No muthafucka!... You told me it was already planned!" She shouted.

"I'm just playing with you."

Totally forgetting to make reservations at a restaurant, Mujahid hurries downstairs to make some type of reservations to accommodate her plans on being entertained.

After trying to get into Benny's which was booked for the next two weeks, Mujahid finally had some better luck with the Blue room. An Italian restaurant that he never thought of visiting because they served too much pork in their dishes. He was desperate, so he had to book the reservations. They had an 8:15 p.m. slot available.

"Perfect... I'll take it!" Mujahid anxiously agreed to. "Mr. and Mrs. Samad is the name." He said arranging and reserving the slot that was open.

Now that that's done, all he has to do now is gather his team to get rid of the work, Mujahid thought to himself.

More importantly, how do he explain all this to Aisha. She's been through a lot in her life. Emotionally she can't take no more heartbreak, or disappointment from Mujahid being taken away from her again. this would have to be handled extremely careful. And assurance was needed to comfort her in believing Mujahid was safe and not in the mix of things.

While lying on the couch with all those thoughts going through his head he suddenly hears Aisha calling him.

"Bay come here!"

"What's up baby?" Mujahid asked in a soft voice.

"So how was your day?" She asked.

But before he could answer she bombarded him with what seemed like a million and one questions.

"Who came to see you?... What they want?... I hope you not ready to do no dumb shit... Cause when you were gone nobody was there but me. And I'm not gone through that shit no more!"

"Nah baby, it's not like that! It was a friend... He offered me a job."

"A job doing what?" She asked in an almost innocent, yet at the same time suspicious tone.

"In the import, export business." Mujahid said trying to stay as close to the truth as possible.

"Okay Bay, I see you moving up in the world." She said in a playful voice.

Little did she know Mujahid was ready to transform into the alter ego she had never seen, Lunatic. She knew he existed, but never witnessed him at play.

1.3 SUPREME TEAM

I t's been three weeks since Mujahid's meeting with Tone.
Instead of jumping in the game head first, he decided to
move at a turtle's pace and carefully plan his attack.

While sitting back absorbing the streets gossip and putting
together an elite no nonsense type squad, he decided that in
order for him to have longevity, he had to be the behind the
scenes cat, using somebody else to be the front man in his
attack. Mujahid began to assemble his pieces and let the reign
commence.

He was by far no dummy. He had always been the streets,
but now it was time to become an avenue.

He goes to a drawer in the end table that sat at the edge of
the sofa he had been planted on. He pulls out a pad and pen and
begins to scribe ferociously nonstop for about an hour.

Once done, he began to read to himself the contents he
had just written at the top of the pad. It was what looked like
elected offices to be held by certain individuals. At the very top
of the page was the words Chairman of the Board. Then under
that was vice president, continuing in a downward motion was
treasurer, secretary, warlord and generals.

Underneath that was mathematical equations, almost like
he was solving, or developing some type of formula. Different
formulas to do whatever it was he intended to do.

After he looked over his work to be sure it was what he
wanted, he picked up the phone and dialed a number.

A few rings later, somebody picks up and conversation
ensues.

"What's up Unc…?" Mujahid said.

Then after a brief pause allowing a response he continues with, "I need to see you A.S.A.P! It's time to shed the shell and get it!... where you at?"

Not able to hear the response on the other end of the phone, one could only speculate the reply from Mujahid's next statement.

"I'm on my way."

Mujahid hangs up the phone and leaves out the front door in route to the destination he had just learned Unc was at.

Unc was his father's youngest brother. He had been out of Mujahid's life all his younger years due to a conviction for the robbery of a McDonalds where he locked everybody in the walk in freezer. It was an inside job that he and a partner of his who had been a manager at the McDonalds had devised.

In the initial plan, it was supposed to had been an in and out job that would net an easy twenty grand. Not a lot of money, but for the 70's that was a jackpot. Anyway, the job didn't go as planned. Circumstances changed the outcome and Unc ended up maxing out a fifteen year bid.

By the time he finally made it home, Mujahid was doing a bid himself.

It was crazy how they ran into one another after the separation.

Mujahid was just coming home from a bid. And as usual running wild. He had kept hearing about this cat named M-100 who was chewing on something kind of heavy. Once Mujahid got out, he decided he had to formally introduce himself to M-100 via a home invasion.

Just as Mujahid gets inside the house and ties everybody up, who but Unc kicks the door in. Not knowing this 6' 2" stocky build man was his uncle he hadn't seen in twenty years, Mujahid let off three shots, two hit Unc. As Unc falls out from the shots to the shoulder and stomach Mujahid exits the house from the back door.

Weeks later, still not fully recovered from the ordeal, Unc walks into the house of Mujahid's mother Big Bren. A 6'1" extremely dark woman with the skills to pay the bills, a first class con artist.

At first sight Mujahid's reaction was to draw his ratchet. And he did.

"Hold up... What's going on?" Big Bren asked trying to understand why Mujahid was trippin.

"You know him mom?" Mujahid asks in a confused yet volatile state.

She laughed and said, "That's Khalil boy!... That's your uncle."

"My unc!" Almost paralyzed from the shock of her statement, Mujahid goes on to ask, "Who his peoples?"

"Thats your dad's baby brother! You can't tell... They look just alike." She replies in a jolly tone.

With a smile on his face, Unc just embraced Mujahid and praised how much like his father he was. They talked, never discussing the details of the incident that lead them to the point Mujahid felt he had to draw his pistol on him.

From that day on they were like brothers. Unc had lost his youth to the penitentiary, so he felt as though he could regain his youth through the activities of his nephew Mujahid. On a quest to regain his youth Unc stuck to Mujahid like siamese twins.

Arriving at the destination Mujahid had set out to reach, he was greeted by a light skin burly type fellow he addressed as Unc.

"What's the situation?" Unc asks.

"I got a connect that's gone flood me with whatever I want. I'm ready to get it again. But I need you to play boss hog. I can't afford for my name to be spoken in these streets.

I already put together a plan... All I need is for you to be my hands, ears and face. You wit me?" Mujahid asks anticipating a response that would give himself the green light to say go.

You already know I'm on board with whatever with you. We family!... We pump the same blood... So you know I'm gone to the death with you." Unc said with all the emotions one could possess for his kin.

"First thing I need you to do is not say nothing to nobody! Let me do all the talking... You just sit back and let me put shit in effect."

Not understanding the request made by Mujahid, Unc agreed to it. And trusted Mujahid knew what he was doing.

"Let's go." Mujahid insisted.

Making an adventure out of the day, they spent the rest of the day journeying around the city of Philadelphia meeting and greeting people from all walks of life. The whole time Unc never uttered a word. But at the same time Mujahid was getting his name out to the masses.

Before you knew it Unc was a household name. All through the streets his name rang bells, bomb ass work at reasonable prices.

Mujahid's plan was to flood the city with weight. And set up shop in the suburbs, where the prices were higher and the quantity was smaller, but at the same prices as the city.

Mujahid had gotten his brother Raheem to overlook all the work on the streets. He held the position as general. Raheem was 6' 8", 278 pounds solid. A boxer and basketball player. Lazy in life, but hungry for money to feed his family.

By this time Raheem had three kids by Aisha's younger sister Muffy.

Mujahid knew he had to keep Raheem far away as possible in order for his pillow talk not to reach Aisha.

Though all the chaos she still wasn't aware of Mujahid's reentry in the game.

Mujahid set it up whereas, Raheem believes he's providing a service for Unc.

His duties only entailed making sure all locations are always operating 24 hours a day, collecting money from these spots and scouting out new locations to conquer. At a minimum, he sees five grand a week pay.

Then there's J.A.P.A.N, also referred to as Hafiz. This is Mujahid's middle brother above Raheem. Not quite as tall or stocky, but wore his heart on his sleeve. Standing only 6' 6", 240 pounds. He was more of a slender type dude. In a chair from an altercation that left him paralyzed in the early 90's. A stone cold killer and manipulator of minds. Even from his chair he still demanded, as well as received, the utmost respect from the streets.

Sitting in a chair never stopped his quest to do him. Hafiz became the warlord.

Although he was Mujahid's brother, this was someone Mujahid had to keep near. Not out of love, but out of caution. For some reason Hafiz resented Mujahid. He tried his best to conceal his resentment, but it was so deeply rooted that he couldn't help but to let it be seen.

He was creeping with Mujahid's baby mom. Hafiz felt he had to keep this hidden, but Mujahid knew. He just didn't care. Hafiz tried his hardest to conceal this little dark secret.

However, his right hand man and first cousin to both brothers, Hafiz and Mujahid, was Shaq. A 6'7" 255 pound

G.O.rilla in every sense of the word. From looks to actions. But his passion was getting money.

A hustler for real. He shed light on the darkness of the whispers.

If a dollar was to be made Shaq was on it.

He had been raised with Mujahid and Hafiz. So he was more like a brother than a cousin. He was always around when Mujahid made a move until finally Mujahid took and put him under his wing, molded him. And in the end Shaq was loyal to Mujahid for giving him the game in the rawest form.

Shaq, in Mujahid's plan became the treasurer. His only duty was to be sure the count on the money came up straight and even. He turned it into Unc, who was a vice president, who in turn turned it over to Mujahid.

Once Mujahid got it, he divided it up and made sure the connect money was always where it was supposed to be when it had to be there.

Mujahid had worked so hard to see the team he put together do their jobs and eat like their stomachs had no bottoms. But at the same time monopolize the drug trade in Philadelphia.

14 MATRIMONY

Everything was running smoothly on the streets. Mujahid and Aisha was closer than ever in their relationship.

In fact, it was to the point Mujahid had wanted to show his appreciation and love for Aisha. And he wanted the world to witness it.

One day while spending quality time with Aisha, Mujahid sweating nervously and scared, finally gathers up the courage to ask for her hand in marriage.

Mujahid had always dreamed of the day he would do the deed of proposing. The way he would hope it go down never even came close to the actual equation of how it was actually done.

After a night out, entertained by dinner and a movie, roses and a carriage ride though the city, absorbing the sights and enjoying the moment they shared together, Mujahid reached into his jacket pocket to get the ring he had brought.

A 3.5 karat pink diamond surrounded by blue gems. When suddenly he realized he had left it in his jacket pocket of the outfit he had on earlier in that day.

In all the commotion of getting ready and being slightly late due to the business affairs that ran a little long, he totally forgot to bring the ring.

Although the setting was perfect for such an occasion, it wasn't going to happen this night.

After a beautiful night cap at a quiet little upscale bar down Society Hill, this was an atmosphere where money was the only common link the inhabitants of this area shared, Mujahid and Aisha left for a final detour to their home.

Upon arriving at their residence Aisha wanted sex, but didn't alert Mujahid of her intentions. So prior to getting their Aisha had called ahead and had her younger sister Najah set the tone.

After opening the door Mujahid was automatically taken aback by the aroma left behind as they entered the house. It was a sweet, yet pleasant smell.

There were no lights on. Therefore, the contents that awaited still remained to be seen.

Mujahid clicked on the light and was instantly filled with the sentiments of love.

Aisha had rose petals completely covering the floor and steps leading into the bedroom. Beside the bed was a nightstand with all types of edible treats, oils and toys. Music lightly serenading Mujahid's ears with melodic tunes of baby making music.

Aisha gently holds him from behind at the waist and kisses the nape of his neck. Still standing there amazed by the efforts Aisha put into the ambiance of the evening, Mujahid thought to himself, I got to make love to her like I never did in my life.

He slowly reaches back and grabs her from behind.

"Come here baby." Were the only words he managed to utter.

Then after a few seconds of embracing the softness of Aisha's body, he began to speak.

"All this for me?... That's why I love you so much." Also managed to escaped his mouth as well.

Filled with so many emotions they began to undress one another.

Until finally standing before one another just as they entered the world, naked.

Unlike normal nights, or episodes of their love making, Aisha took charge. She pushed Mujahid down onto the bed and took complete control of the tempo. Kissing him gently down his chiseled bronze body, stopping only to take his dick into her mouth.

But before she fully engulfed his dick, she lightly nibbled on the head of it sending him into a paralyzing shocked mode.

The sensation was so intense that Mujahid bussed two shots before even touching the pussy. Not to worry cause before he had the chance to retreat to a limp state, Aisha was all over him making sure his member was at full attention once again.

She straddled him and road into the sunset, bucking like a filly until every ounce of fluid had been spilling from Mujahid's body.

Normally they would roll over and distance themselves from the activity to ensure sleep would be peaceful. However, this night Aisha just laid down on Mujahid's chest still mounted on his dick and slept so peaceful.

Unable to wait, after an hour of sleep, Mujahid had to wake Aisha up and pop the question.

"Baby... Baby... Wake up, it's important." Was all that could be heard over top of the buzzing of Aisha's snoring.

Still shaking her until she was awake, Mujahid got up and got the ring from the pocket of the jacket he had forgotten earlier.

Concealed so that she couldn't see it and spoke, "Baby I love you!... Since your existence in my world I feel like you've become an asset as well as a compliment to my life! There's nothing I want more than to have you as my wife, so I'm asking ..."

But before he could get the question out, a "Yes" was in the makings being screamed by Aisha.

Instead of waiting until the next morning, she immediately began to call her family and friends. Waking everybody up with the news of their engagement.

Within a matter of weeks they were married.

1.5 SWITCH UP

Now officially Mrs. Abdus-Samad, Mujahid felt it was his duty to clue Aisha in on his business. Both worlds, the legit ventures and underworld dealings.

After doing so, not even a full six months after their marriage, Aisha felt betrayed.

At the same time she allowed greed to embrace and welcome the deceitfulness into her hidden agenda.

By this time Mujahid is up. He incorporated himself and business ventures. He now owns and operates a van service that services the entire state of Pennsylvania prison system, real estate, a management label, a clothing line was in the making. Not to mention two night clubs he owns. Life couldn't be any better for him or so he believed.

A few more months into their marriage the attitudes have changed. Aisha no longer plays her part as before.

She's now more focused on the underworld dealings than the actual task of spending money. It's almost like she to the point where she trying to be a boss lady or something.

She's now on some type of quest to become an influence within the circle of the underworld.

Not realizing the motive beset within the realms of Aisha's head, Mujahid continues to school, mold and prepare Aisha for the game. Just in case of emergency. After all he still on parole. So a free man he couldn't be which was in part why he structured his layout as he did.

As with all dealings in the game, Mujahid used his wife's name as a front. This way he could operate quietly under the radar of all the agencies and bureaus that took pride in running down and destroying the lives of those not as fortunate enough as those born with a silver spoon to prosper.

Just as Mujahid was breaking down the structure of his operation for Aisha, he receives a phone call on that special phone he was giving by Tone.

"What's the math?" He asks as he answered the calling of his livelihood.

"I'll call you back."

Before Mujahid could even let Tone know he acknowledged the call, the phone went dead. Odd behavior even for Tone.

Not paying it no mind, Mujahid begins to gather all the money he has for Tone.

He leaves his home and goes to a pay phone. He immediately calls Unc to collect the last couple drops from Shaq.

"What's up Unc?... Take the milk out the window."

This was the code to alert Unc to empty the safe he held in his apartment.

"No problem." Was all that was said by Unc.

Within a matter of 20–30 minutes Unc arrives at Mujahid's house with a briefcase containing three million dollars.

Along with the briefcase came a problem that shouldn't have even made it as far as Mujahid.

There was a crew from New Jersey trying to set up shop in the area already occupied by the family.

"Unc, call Hafiz and give him the run down. Have him send his team through to cease the move before it erupts into all out chaos.

I got a meeting to attend, so I'll get back to you later to check the solution." Was all Mujahid said before exiting his home to meet with Tone.

Upon arriving at the Bellevue Stratton hotel to meet with Tone, the set up was all but normal.

As usual, Mujahid stops at the concierge desk to ask for Anthony

Austin, gets the room number and goes up to the room designated for this meeting.

As Mujahid was about to knock on the door, it opens on its own. You can tell it wasn't fully closed by the way it swayed with the wind from the balcony being open.

Mujahid calls out, "Tone... It's Mujahid."

Rather than Tone responding to the call, a cat he had never seen exits the side room.

"Please... Be seated." He said.

Then proceeded to say, "My name is Tito. I'm your new contact. The layout remains the same, the players just switched positions to keep the heat down. Tone still around, just at a new location. He sends his love. He's told me of the beautiful job you've been doing."

It kind of bothered Mujahid that Tone would change up on him so abruptly without even warning him, or giving him a heads up of the switch up.

Deep down Mujahid just wanted to get the work his empire relied on to function. So he hands over his briefcase to this Tito cat.

In return Tito hands Mujahid a laundry bag with the usual work at the same price.

Unlike Tone, Tito utters, "See you next month."

Which Mujahid felt to be strange due to the fact Tone never sets a date or time frame, he just shows up. Something about this new guy was off key.

Without saying anything Mujahid just smiled with a nod to express the sentiments of okay in response to this statement made by Tito. Then leaves the room to get back to his normal functions of his day.

Before Mujahid even gets out of the hotel his phone rings.

Once he answered it, he heard, "Nephew we got a situation!... The problem I addressed you with struck blood."

"I'm on my way!" Was Mujahid's response.

After dropping off his material he had just scored, Mujahid headed to Unc's house and was briefed as to the details of the situation.

16 NOT HEEM

Once fully informed of the details Mujahid calls a meeting to combat the situation at hand.

It seems war has been threatened by some cats who didn't belong in the state of Pennsylvania. Yet alone on the block that handsomely contributed to the majority of the family's income.

"Did you call Hafiz like I told you?" Mujahid asks Unc.

"Not yet... Before I had the chance to Raheem called me to say, Auburn Street was hit heavy... Without even thinking I naturally called you." Unc responds.

Mujahid had to take a moment to realize Unc wasn't a thinker. Or a take charge type dude unless forced to do so. After all, he only supposed to be the face of the family. Mujahid was the brains of the operation.

Without further delay Mujahid calls Hafiz to rally the men. War has been waged.

"As Salaamu Alaikum... Where you at?" asked Mujahid in a calm but very authoritative voice.

"Downtown 55th." He replies.

"Gather your squad, time to make it happen." Said Mujahid.

"Whats up?" Asked Hafiz.

"Just meet me on Rush street A.S.A.P." Mujahid urged.

Rush street was a block where the family kept nothing but artillery. It was the block opposite of Auburn street.

Already in route to Rush street Mujahid phones ahead to Raheem to have him meet him there.

Just as Mujahid pulls up he sees a white Jeep Cherokee pull up beside Raheem and unload what sounded like a thousand cannons into his frame.

Laying in a pool of blood unable to move, Raheem gasping for air, raises his left hand to motion for help.

While the Jeep was speeding off, Mujahid hurried to Raheem to comfort his baby brother. From the way he was bleeding, it was no saving him. Even still Mujahid yelled for somebody to call an ambulance.

Holding Raheem's head in his lap, Mujahid just sat there rocking back and forth with tears streaming down his face.

As Hafiz and his team pulled up, the block was flooded with cops, ambulances and news reporters, so they kept it moving. Not aware that it was his baby brother who all the attention was for, Hafiz calls Mujahid's phone.

Unable to reach him, Hafiz parks at the bottom of the block and sends one of his goons up to the top of the block to see what had happened.

Within minutes his goon reported back and tells Hafiz, "Your brother got rocked."

Deep down inside Hafiz had hoped it was Mujahid, but became instantly broken up inside to learn it was Raheem.

At a loss of words, Hafiz pauses before attempting to call Mujahid once again.

This time the call is placed and received.

"Hafiz..." But before Mujahid could finish his statement Hafiz asks, "What the fuck just happened?"

"It was a blast and roll. Just as I was hitting the block I seen the work being done." Mujahid said.

"Who was it?" Hafiz asked.

Ali, who was Raheem's first lieutenant, informed Mujahid that it was those Jersey cats.

Raheem told them they couldn't set up shop on this block, referring to Auburn street. Words were exchanged and Raheem wound up dead, that was the end result of the squabble.

"So where they at? Who their peoples? Who brought them here? Who they take orders from?" All questions asked by Hafiz.

1.7 BLOOD SHED

several weeks later, just as in any hood throughout the world, the streets began to talk. Except in this case, they were singing in attempts of appraisal. Everybody and their mother had been in their bag of tricks trying to collect on the 50 grand Mujahid put out for information as to the whereabouts of the boys who killed his little brother Raheem.

Finally, through all the whispering and rumors, information surfaced. And from a reliable source.

It seems the boys that struck blood and signed their death warrant was the family of Jabbar.

Jabbar was a nobody. A low level petty hustler. A has been that never was. He abandoned the hustling game to become a stick up kid. He had a nice sting for 80 grand and a couple kilos and tried to bounce back on the scene.

Just as so many times before, he fucked that money and work up, ended up trying his hand at plating cars. Not knowing the crew he linked up with already was under surveillance. Basically he walked into a situation blindly.

Anyhow, word on the street is that he came home and decided to rent Auburn street to those Jersey cats. It seems he brokered a deal that would Net him 10% of the total profits that was made in a week. As well as, a connect that would flood him with dope.

Never dealing in heroin in his life, he was out his league, but he still wanted to try his hand.

The reliable source had appeared to be the woman of Jabbar. Or at least he believed her to be.

She was a whore who sucked and fucked to get next to the biggest bank roll by the name of Sierra.

A short, big titty, well built, pretty bitch, who had no goals, or ambitions in life, except to wake up every morning with get high. No matter what the get high was, she wanted it.

One can only speculate as to the abuse suffered in her life that she appears to be hiding so poorly.

Sierra was trying to land a bank roll affiliated with the family.

Just as any bitch does who wants to be noticed, she cuts into Shaq. And before you knew it, she spilled the beans. In her case it was more like emptied the can.

She was tired of the on again off again hustling lifestyle Jabbar had.

The heat from the killing of Raheem has him scared to surface. He had a little bread to last a few weeks. But without any money coming in, he was fucked up in the game.

As with any tender dick nigga, he couldn't and wouldn't accept the fact that Sierra wasn't exclusively his. She chased bank rolls and got high. With him not getting no money, she was back on the prowl.

Sierra heard about the 50 grand and immediately called Shaq.

Instead of being responsible and take care of business first, she tried to back door Shaq and bit off more than she could chew.

Once Shaq gorilla fucked her, she was stuck. Her intentions were to get Shaq open and then weasel her way into the circle of the family.

Things didn't quite work themselves out as she had planned. Instead of working her way in, she actually ousted her chances of ever being tied to an elite circle in the eyes of Shaq.

A bitch like Sierra without morals, or values wasn't capable of possessing the one thing needed to enter his circle. And that was loyalty.

She had not a clue of what it was to be loyal to a muthafucka. She was a scavenger. Not worthy of swallowing the cum from his balls.

In Shaq's plan this bitch played a vital part.

Now with the data on Jabbar's whereabouts and schedule of his daily movements, Shaq brought the information back to Mujahid.

Only after he researched the contents of Sierra's story to find out if it held any weight. And just as she had detailed Jabbar's movements, it was like clockwork, every move, twist, turn and breath he took was accounted for.

After sitting on Jabbar for almost a month, Shaq finally decides to put the plan in effect. In order for it to be executed to perfection Sierra had to play her part.

Sprung over the thought of Shaq blessing her with the dick, she had by this time became obsessed with, Sierra takes the bait and becomes the smoke screen to carry out a clean hit on Jabbar.

The plan was to force Sierra's hand in creating an altercation with Jabbar. This way his love for the bitch could force him to chase the whore down. Therefore, letting his guard down.

With Sierra not coming home. And when she does allow herself to be seen, she's in and out, no rap.

To Jabbar this is strange behavior for Sierra. Especially now that he believes she's pregnant by him carrying his first born son.

Back in the game, feeling like the heat from the hit on Raheem has gone undetected as well as unanswered, Jabbar again opens up shop. This time on the Southside of Philadelphia.

He surrounds himself with cats he felt would kill a brick if he commanded. His swagger has returned and the cockiness of his actions is now fully noticed by all who comes into contact with this joker.

His love for Sierra would be his downfall.

Sierra pulls up on Jabbar and states to him, "I'm having an abortion, don't call my phone, don't send word through the circle of my girlfriends, It's over!"

Now fucked up mentally, feeling like his world has just came crumbling down on him, Jabbar grabs and slaps the bullshit out of her.

He takes her keys out of the car ignition and tries to carry her in the house in attempts to persuade her not to leave him. And that he was really in love with her ass.

Watching all this go down was a goon of Hafiz by the name of Kenyatta.

Already in place, waiting for the commotion to go down. Kenyatta intervenes and tries to help Sierra.

"You alright shorty?" Was the words he spoke in an almost cocky tone.

"No! He won't let me leave! Can you please call the cops?"

Sierra asked this man in an innocent but scared tone. Also adding, "He put his hands on me." Now yelling and crying at the same time, "Look at my face!" pointing to the bruise that appeared on her face.

"You did this to me." She said wiping the blood from her nose and spitting blood from her mouth.

Before the spit she spat could hit the ground, two shots reigned out into the head of Jabbar from a .45 Ruger.

The team that Jabbar felt would protect him just so happened to be the up and coming goons hoping to tie into Hafiz's clique.

As if nothing ever happened, Kenyatta slid off into the winds of the air.

Shocked and scared, Sierra spat on the body of Jabbar. And then took back her car keys and sped off.

Before she could hit the corner of the block, a car pulls beside her and let another two shots into her vehicle then sped off.

Just as Hafiz wanted, no witnesses left behind.

Sierra had been a liability.

Shaq just needed her to bring Jabbar out of hiding.

Once she played her role, it was planned for her to be eliminated.

She was better off dead then breathing the same oxygen as Shaq. He felt as if he was sharing air with a germ of chemical warfare. Her lack of loyalty was a major sin in the sea of deception. And detrimental to mankind everywhere.

18 SLEEPING WITH THE ENEMY

till not content with the death of Jabbar, Mujahid still wants the soul of the one who executed the hit.

Now was the time to implement phase two of the plan.

In this elaborate scheme, the team from Jersey was tracked down to a small block off Broadway in Camden, New Jersey.

Just as Jabbar was being watched, so was the family of the kid by the name of Belly who killed Raheem.

Belly's baby mother was a dancer by name of Almond who worked out of a hole in the wall strip club called, The Tender Trap. Located on Broadway and Division, a section of the city known to be on the cuff of downtown and the adjoining section of the city known as Centerville.

Belly was a nobody who was working hard to elevate in rank within the crew he ran with known as the Sons of Malcolm X.

A rather small clique trying to expand outside the confines of Camden.

They met Jabbar during his eight year bid. He sold them dreams of being a boss in Philly.

Upon Jabbar's release he resumed contact with Jamal. This was who ran the Sonz of Malcolm X.

Together they incorporated a plan to bring them outside the folds of Jersey and into the mainstream of a major city.

On a quest to prove his ability to head a team, Belly stepped up and headed the team that drew first blood on the family. Now it's time for the piper to pay the cost of his flute blowing.

It was close to 2 a.m. almost time for the Tender Trap to close for the evening.

All night a cat by the name of Jahlil, planted by Hafiz, was really indulging in flirtatious activity with Almond. Had it been different circumstances, Jahlil would of definitely took shorty serious. She was nice!

About 5'3", 135-140 pounds, coco complexion with long silky hair.

You could tell by her beautiful features that she was mixed with something.

Jahlil's guess would be Spanish or Italian.

It was something about her chinky eyes that spoke volumes. Almost like it was a sin to body a bitch this bad.

Just as the bar was closing, Jahlil asks Almond, "Can I feed you?... No strings attached. If money is a problem...I'll pay the fee for your time and company."

Flashing a mitt that had to be about 5-10 grand, not counting the stack and a half she made from him alone that night.

All night she was held hostage by Jahlil. For some strange reason she felt she knew Jahlil, like there had actually been a connection between the two. For Jahlil, it was business. However, for Almond it was pure attraction to the dollar signs in Jahlil's hand.

She agreed to allow him to take her out after work to a 24hour diner on Admiral Wilson Boulevard.

They got together. They ate, talked and ended up getting a motel room.

Just as a gentleman would do, Jahlil insisted on a room with two beds.

But Almond wanted to be fucked by this man she felt had what it took to quench the urges she craved.

Normally after a night of dancing, Almond doesn't want to be bothered with the bullshit of having a nigga jumping up and down on her.

Unlike the normal, she was really feeling Jahlil. And under the posterity that said it's only business, Jahlil felt a spark for her as well.

Upon entering the room, Jahlil was attacked by the physical of Almond. She pushed him against the door and immediately began to unleash her passion.

Pushing her away, Jahlil demanded her to be easy, as well as gentle.

Although this was gone be her last night to enjoy life, Jahlil felt it was his duty to pleasure her one last time. This way she can leave this Earth with a smile on her face. And her body drained of all the juices begging to be released.

Jahlil grabs her from the back of her head with his fingers intertwined in the softness of her silky hair and pulls her near.

Kissing her gently, he lays her upon the bed on her back and proceeds to kiss, lick and soothe her body up and down, until reaching the tips of her toes.

Gently placing them into his mouth and giving each toe its own massage with his tongue.

Allowing the wetness of his tongue to lick up her legs reaching the inner part of her thighs.

Gently biting from the middle of her thighs until he reaches the point of origin where the flames are burning.

As he works his way upward, via the inner thighs, he kisses the lips of her pretty little pussy.

Forgetting his mission momentarily and unleashing all the emotions his soul was capable of possessing, he parts the lips of what he felt was the prettiest pussy he'd ever seen. And allows his tongue to bathe the clitoris with the moisture of his mouth.

Letting the air from his words spoken lightly to mix with the wetness he has just showered her with as he whispered, "Ummmm... you taste so good Almond."

Shaking frantically, Almond begs Jahlil to fuck her.

Before he actually penetrates the hole of her eternal flame, he licks up her stomach to suck the pretty brown nipples of her perky breast.

Biting, pulling and pinching to create a special sensation, while he let the head and shaft of his dick rub against the lips and shell of her pussy.

Begging to the point tears are in her eyes, Almond wants to feel Jahlil's massive manhood enter her immediately.

Swaying her hips in a grinding motion, she finally lines up her pussy to catch the head of Jahlil's dick. And manipulates its movement to slide in her yearning pussy.

As his dick penetrates and stretches the mouth of her pussy open, all you could hear was a gasp for air and a few moans demanding in a rage of passion to "Fuck me Daddy!... Give it to me!"

As commanded, Jahlil fucks her with all the passion a nigga could offer to a bitch he felt was destined to be his.

Just as she was about to let out the biggest orgasm of her life, Jahlil takes his dick out from within the flames and teases Almond.

Sliding in and out repeatedly with no more than the girth of the head of his tool penetrating her.

Now hotter than ever and ready to release this built up orgasm, Jahlil flips her over and long strokes her in a hard and fast motion.

Being sure to allow her to feel every inch of him as he traveled the depths of her brewing volcano until she begins to quiver and gasp for air from the intensity of her orgasm.

Soon as Jahlil was about to peak, he draws his pistol, a glock .40 and lets the first of two shots pierce through the back of her head.

As her body lay there limp and bleeding, he came on her. Then gets up and leaves.

Before exiting, he blows a kiss and utters, "Had it been different circumstances you would of been mines."

Then drifts off into the wee hours of the early morning.

19. BACK IN THE BING

Meanwhile, Mujahid was awaiting the news the task had been fulfilled.

At home regretting he had ever met Aisha. He lights a Newport then just snaps on Aisha.

She had been bitching all night at him over petty shit, almost like she was trying to provoke Mujahid to react in a violent manner.

Unwilling to accommodate the assumption, he goes downstairs to his den to escape the rants of the mad woman.

Just as he opens the door to his den the news he was awaiting is trying to get to him. Hearing the phone ring, he hurries into his den and answers the phone to get the data he had been awaiting.

"Mission complete." Was all that was said before the line went dead.

Without any more words being spoken he hung up the phone and took a seat at his desk smiling, feeling joy and pleasure from the pain and strife that was soon to befall Belly and his kid.

Later on that day Mujahid awakens to an empty house. Without notice, Aisha had gotten up and left, leaving her whereabouts a mystery, But also a breath of fresh air for Mujahid.

He proceeds with the activities normally done when he has to visit his parole man.

He showers, get dressed and leave for the trip to the parole office.

While driving he receives a call from Aisha.

At first wanting to ignore it, he pressed the ignore button.

Unwilling to accept the fact Mujahid wasn't available, she proceeded to call back to back until he answered.

"As salammu alaikum..."

Without even returning the salutations, Aisha just immediately began to fuss.

"You ignoring me now pussy!" She yelled angrily.

"Nah... I was on the expressway and my phone fell under the seat... I had to come off to get it from under there." He said knowing it was a lie.

Aisha went on for about 15 minutes about shit he had no clue of what she was talking about until finally she says, "You gone get yours pussy!" then just hung up.

Within 5 minutes of the parole office Mujahid didn't even attempt to call her back.

Instead he decided he'd do it once he leaves the parole office.

He pulls up, still bothered by what Aisha was saying trying to figure out what the fuck she was talking about.

As he's ready to enter the building he sees a white van pull up.

The driver gets out and began to untangle a crate full of chains and shackles.

As always a small drop of fear over took him, not because of his wrong doings, but because there's always a possibility he could return back to prison for the slightest thing.

It all depended upon the mood the parole officer was in.

He could have not gotten any pussy last night, wife made him mad, now he has an attitude.

Highly unlikely due to the relationship Mujahid had with his P.O.

He was a young dude, no more than 27 years old. He thought he was the hippest thing since sliced bread. Therefore, Mujahid catered to his ego.

Mujahid had a way of using words, actions and gestures to win over people. Especially those white folks who held his freedom within their hands.

Without giving it another thought Mujahid signs in and waits to be seen by his P.O.

While at the sign in window he hears Mrs. Tasha, the receptionist at the sign in desk, page Mr. Gross, his P.O.

He immediately calls back. And Mrs.Tasha shuts the sliding glass to speak in private to him.

Still not worried Mujahid takes a seat.

Although there were several people ahead of him to see Mr. Gross, after about ten minutes of waiting, Mr. Gross comes out to the waiting area and calls out, "Mr. Abdu-Samad."

Looking around Mujahid says, "I'm not next, it's people ahead of me."

Mr. Gross replies, "They still gone be seen whether first or last, let me deal with them. Now come on back."

Mujahid got up and followed Mr. Gross back to his office.

Thinking he wanted a urine sample Mujahid began to unfasten his pants and asks, "Where the cup at?"

"For what?" Mr. Gross replied.

"You don't want no piss this trip?" Mujahid inquired.

"No, have a seat." In a serious toned voice was ordered by Mr. Gross.

He walks out of the office and returns with three big hillbillies. They were some huge ass white boys.

"Put your hands behind your back!" One of them said.

"For what?" Mujahid ask in a high pitched puzzled tone.

"Put your hands behind your back sir! This the last time I'm telling you." was heard before they rushed in and attacked Mujahid.

Wrestled down to the floor and shackled, Mujahid was snapping.

"Calm down." Was said by Mr. Gross.

"My supervisor wants to see you" also followed the last statement.

Sitting there waiting for about 5 minutes, mad as hell at the situation that was going down, Mujahid asks, "What's all this about?"

Before Mr. Gross could answer, in comes the supervisor Mr. Norton.

"Is it anything you want to tell me?" He asks.

"Nah! if I did I would have been said it." Mujahid said in a very hostile and agitated tone.

"Well we have reports from a Mrs. Johnson..."

Cutting Mr. Norton off, Mujahid corrects the name, "It's Johnston" Mujahid said.

"And that's my wife."

Mr. Norton proceeded to inform Mujahid that Aisha had reported him to the P.O.'s office for engaging in illegal distribution of narcotics.

Fucked up mentally, as well as emotionally, Mujahid couldn't say nothing. He was hurt.

Jail is a place I wouldn't send my worst enemy, so for her to do this only meant she no longer had love for me anymore, Mujahid thought to himself.

All Mujahid could do was put his head down and shed a tear. Not because he was going back to jail, but because it was behind something Aisha said. The one he loved and took vows to provide for.

PART TWO

AISHA S TAKEOVER

2.1 THE SET—UP

Now with Mujahid out of the way, Aisha was free to do her as deemed fit.

Taught by the best, she decided to keep the family operating, but at a more productive pace. So she believed.

For the next few weeks she ruled heavy. And with an iron fist.

Beginning to feel the loneliness and sentiments of love missed by Mujahid, Aisha begins to wild out.

She started smoking weed heavy, popping pills and drinking like a fish.

She had yet to commit adultery.

Still wanting to be with Mujahid, she would think to herself, how could she make amends and put her life back together without retaliation for her actions.

She never wanted to see Mujahid caged up within the belly of the beast. She was so emotional, due to the fact she had been hearing through the whispers of the streets that Mujahid had gotten this little hood rat by the name of Kedah pregnant.

Unable to bear anymore children, she felt a certain type way.

She had always hoped that she would be the one to birth Mujahid's seed.

If this wasn't possible, she had a backup plan to adopt.

Rather than have factual proof to support the allegations she had harbored for some time now, she shut down and became cold as ice towards her husband. Without even confronting him to find truth in the rumors that echoed through her soul as the winds in a ghost town did. She just reacted in the worst possible way within the eyes of Mujahid.

Although Kedah was a stallion, built like a brick shit house, ass fatter than buffy the body and softer than cotton. She had the resemblance to Sanaa Lathan mixed with Latoya Luckett. Mujahid did fuck with her on a regular basis. However, she was in no way pregnant by him. This was just a silly rumor started by Makeebah to cause conflict between Aisha and Mujahid.

Makeebah was a homie of both Mujahid and Aisha who at one time or another fucked both of them.

She was in the eyes of the public, more of the butch type dyke.

A deep chocolate, big breasted, fat ass homie, who hid her physique through the bagginess of oversized sweats, jeans and saggy clothing.

Her persona warranted the characteristics of a man, but deep down had the urges of a woman in need of a nice dick to at times, to calm her hormones.

Always around Mujahid and Aisha she naturally took a liking to both.

She had been Aisha's first and only bi-sexual experience before meeting Mujahid.

As well as a late night jump off for Mujahid on several occasions.

Never really taking Makeebah as a serious bitch or somebody worthy of a relationship, Mujahid looked at her as a homie.

They partied many bitches together, clubbed, hung out just chillin. It never once crossed his mind that she even desired men on a serious basis. Never letting on to the fact she had a crush on Mujahid and felt a certain type way by his decision to marry Aisha.

Makeebah harbored resentment toward Aisha. Through small minute actions she allowed her resentment to seep out into the open chatters of the streets. Knowing that Mujahid was fucking Kedah, she began to circulate a rumor of pregnancy for the sole purpose of putting a wedge between Aisha and Mujahid. And Aisha bit the bait.

2.2 RIGHTING HER WRONG

N ow left all alone, Aisha takes it upon herself to make things right.

The only thing Mujahid loved besides Aisha, was money. And the only thing he feared more than dying alone, was being broke. So Aisha took the teachings of Mujahid and executed to perfection the existence of her presence as his replacement until he returned.

After Mujahid got sent back to the bing, Aisha went and picked up his belongings from the parole office. She also found in the glove compartment of his car, the phone Tone had given him to handle business.

Unaware of who she had to meet, or when she had to meet the connect, she calls the number in the phone.

Unlike Tone, this new cat Tito answers and begins to speak as if he knew Aisha. And what she wanted.

She explained to him that Mujahid was unavailable. Also that he gave her the phone to continue business. And in fact she was his wife.

"Cool with me." Was all Tito said.

Now plugged in, Ashia felt a little sigh of relief that she was able to prove to Mujahid that his departure wouldn't be in vain.

Aware of the procedures of how to get with the connect and where to meet him at, as well as who to ask for, was already learned by her from going with Mujahid a few times.

She had already known the hotel. Plus, she had heard Mujahid say Tones name, so she was all ready to do business.

Business was poppin. And shit still was running smoothly for the next few months.

Aisha got with Unc and used him as her muscle to avoid the alpha males from trying to take advantage of her female characteristics.

Unable to speak to Mujahid, the family had no idea that Aisha was in fact the rat who had him booked.

Without saying so, she knew that if they knew this detail her life would almost be guaranteed to be taken.

She concocted a crazy story of how the administration at the institution where Mujahid was being housed restricted his contact to just immediate family… wife and kids only, due to disciplinary problems.

Without any questions asked, they all fed into this story and protected her as if she was really in power by choice of Mujahid.

Ready to put her spin on things, Aisha stepped her game up and elevated the level of intensity.

She formed her own team with the same structure as the family, with the exception that all her players were females.

Still unaware of the deception Makeebah unleashed that made Aisha surrender her innocence, Aisha gets with Makeebah and takes her under her wing. Sort of like her right hand.

To Makeebah this idea was kind of ludicrous to think that the streets would respect Aisha after the deed she done by sending Mujahid to jail.

Filled with all the love possible for Mujahid, Makeebah accepts the position.

In her mind, she was keeping tabs on Aisha, this was her chance to finally get rid of her. And again become the object of Mujahid's affection.

As many times before, Makeebah constantly says to herself, if only she had put her cards on the table and expressed her feelings to Mujahid, he may not of been so quick to choose Aisha as his soul mate.

Unable to change what's been done with the choice he made, she decided to just rid Mujahid of Ashia for good.

As time progressed Makeebah became the voice behind the newly formed team of bitches.

Aisha was the brains, but it was Makeebah who carried out orders and planted seeds.

In the streets Makeebah had a reputation for cutting bitches and not taking no shit from women or men. Plus, they had the support of the family to solidify them as a team to be reckoned with.

Back in the bing, stuck in the routine of lapping the yard and planning out ways to kill Aisha, was Mujahid.

His influence out in the world was dominant, so to have her killed would be nothing to do. However, he allowed himself to get caught up emotionally.

For every reason he had to kill her, he rationalized an excuse that provoked her into doing what she did.

The boy had it bad! This was his First time in his life being in love.

He always believed he wasn't capable of getting caught up.

He ridiculed other men who allowed themselves to be bitten by the love bug. Just as he always told them, he had to find a way to shake it off and become one with himself.

The confusion within hindered Mujahid's growth as a man he believed. When actually it was only ripening him as a man.

Back from the yard and into the cave in which he dwells was when Mujahid noticed he had a piece of mail. No return sender, but recognized the writing as Aisha's.

It read:

Dear Mujahid I know you mad at me, but don't be. I miss you! I'm very miserable without you. I find it hard to live with myself after the betrayal I've demonstrated towards you.

Me being a female and emotionally unstable is not a valid enough reason to do what I've done.

You are my other half, my better half. And now that you're gone I feel alone. If I could, I would take back the actions I've rendered. But I can't. I can only live with the guilt of knowing I did this to you.

Since you've come into my life, you've been the best thing that happen to me. You helped me to grow and become a woman in total.

Tomorrow's not promised, but just in case I don't see you, or it, I want you to know I truly love you. And still want to be with you.

If you find it in your heart to forgive me, I would forever be grateful. I'll always be yours, just as you'll always be mines

Love, Aisha

After reading the contents of her letter, Mujahid was even more broken up than before.

It was Just at that moment he realized he still loved her and would still lay his life down to protect hers.

Along with the letter was a money order for $2500.00 and photos of her looking good as a muthafucka.

Mujahid was at a loss of words. All he could do was cry and realize that this was his life.

Regardless of how fucked up it maybe, this is who he took

a vow to love and cherish, in sickness and health, to death do us part. So killing her was out the equation, but chastisement was still in order

Two weeks later after getting his thought's together, Aisha receives a letter in response to her letter.

The first one she had received since Mujahid had been incarcerated.

Just as she use to do before they were married, she anxiously opened it and began to read it.

> *Dear Aisha,*
>
> *In response to your letter, all I can say is, I forgive you. I'll always live with the feeling of betrayal for what you've done. But my heart has spoken. It chose you to be its protector, as well as its holder of its key.*
>
> *I can't say I'm not mad, but understanding I can offer.*
>
> *I realize your emotions for whatever reason played a major part in deciding to do what you've done. However, it's apparent your judgement was cloudy and decision was irrational. Yet still, I love you more than life itself.*
>
> *Upon receiving these few choice words of mines, I hope you don't respond back in writing, but in fact pay me a visit.*
>
> *love always, Mujahid.*

Immediately after reading the letter Aisha hurries up to the institution to see Mujahid.

Nervous as hell, but excited at the same time, she enters the visiting room at the jail and awaits the arrival of Mujahid.

There was electronic sliding doors between the visiting room and what she thought to be the inside of the jail.

As they slid open, her heart began to beat rapidly.

And once fully open three men exited, but to her dismay neither one of them was Mujahid.

While she was watching the door, tapping her feet and biting her nails, she feels a tap on her shoulder. She turns around not wanting to miss Mujahid as he entered the room. She was looking to see the expression on his face to try to speculate as to the type of visit it was gone be for her.

Happy or sad, she was just excited he requested to see her.

As Aisha turns to see who was touching her, who but Mujahid was standing there behind her.

Scared to death, almost like she just seen a ghost. She covers her mouth and gets up to hug Mujahid.

Once she embraced him, she was refusing to let go. She just stood there holding him. And apologizing with enough tears in her face to overflow a river.

Once she let's go they seat themselves. Not a word was being said between them. She held her head down. And Mujahid was just staring at her.

To Aisha the tension feels thick enough to cut with a knife.

Finally Mujahid uses his hand to lift her head from the floor and turns it to face him.

Then breaks the silence.

"So how have you been?"

"Fine." She replies.

No matter what he asks, or says, all her responses are summed up in one word.

Until finally Mujahid asks," What's been going on in your world?"

She takes a deep breath and just gives him the rundown of all the events, from keeping his money coming, to adding to his already existing structure to generate more money.

Extremely proud of what she's done on the outside, she became a regular miss chatter box.

Feeling like she gave him a blow by blow description of what's going on, she quiets down awaiting a response from him.

Instead of commenting on the information she'd just given him, he twirls the hair in his goatee and says, "The balls in your court."

Feeling even more lost than before, but kept the feeling to herself, she thinks to herself, what's that supposed to mean?

Still awaiting some type of approval, or recognition for the work she's done to keep his empire stable and functioning, she finally asks, "Is it anything you feel I should be doing?... or not doing?"

He smiles and says, "Yeah, giving my pussy away!" In a jokingly kind of way.

But the look in his eyes said bitch I'm serious!

For the remainder of the visit they talked intensely about the situation that lead to him being there.

Aisha expressed her feelings of betrayal for what was said and done.

Mujahid assured her that there wasn't any truth in the rumor before they heard, "It is now 1500 hours, all visits are now terminated."

As they made their way to the desk at the front of the visiting room to get her pass to leave, Mujahid whispers in her ear, "Keep up the good work."

She smiled and hugged him just as she did when she first seen him.

He hugged her just as tight, feeling on her soft ass before smacking it. Then walking away from her to return to the inside of the jungle in which he was confined.

2.3 EVIL IS SHE WHO HAS NO LOYALTY

Back on her grind, feeling extremely excited, as well as relieved that she finally got the recognition she desperately sought from Mujahid for a job well done, Aisha receives a phone call from Makeebah.

"Damn, what's got into you? You been floating these last couple days." Makeebah inquires curiously.

"I went and seen Mujahid last week, so I feel good." Aisha stated jollier than ever.

Shocked that Mujahid accepted her visit, Makeebah asked, "What he had to say?"

"He miss me... I'm doing a good job and he love me."

An answer Makeebah could have went without hearing.

Now feeling pressured to make her move before the wedge is fully removed from between Aisha and Mujahid, Makeebah quicky makes up a situation to get Aisha to come to her.

"I got a weight sell for you... And if it goes right they gone need about 5 kilos a pop every trip.

It's my cousin Marquan and his partner Tariq. I told them we could meet them tonight at club Horizon around 9:30...

So are we on or what?" Makeebah asks.

"I ain't know Marquan was on... He always seemed to be like a church boy to me... Not into the streets.

But if you want to do it, let's do it." Aisha said in a nonchalant unenthusiastic tone.

Allowing a moment of silence to be interjected, then adding, "After all it's your peeps... We gone do them right. What we charging them?"

"I told him 22.5 a block... The more he cop the lower the prices get.

Once he hit the 10 status he can rock out for 18.5 a block." Makeebah replied.

Aisha agrees to the terms and then hangs up the phone.

She packs a bag with 5 kilos in it. Then put it in the trunk of her CLK 235 Mercedes.

She then jumps into her Q45 and wound up at the beauty salon for a touch up on her hairdo, pedicure and manicure.

"Then later to Daffy's to cop a new outfit to hit the club for her meeting this evening.

Just as Mujahid did, she felt it was her duty to always look her best in the presence of customers.

With her hair tossed up in a New Age Bob with burgundy highlights, a Lenny Austin pants suit in an off white color.

A burgundy silk sheer blouse and minolo's latest six inch heels in an egg shell white color. Plus, her crystal fox mink to set it off.

Two karat diamonds in her ears. Her wedding rock on her finger. She was stunting super heavy.

Ready to meet and greet, she calls Makeebah.

"What's up, you ready?" She asks in an excited to be seen type tone.

Makeebah replies, "Ready for what, it's only Marquan and Tariq... They ain't nobody to floss for."

They was family to Makeebah, but customers to Aisha, so she felt the need to look the part.

"Whateva... You ready or not?" Aisha asks again.

"Yeah, I need you to slide through and scoop me... I'm at my aunt Nita's up Abbottsford.

When you get close call and I'll come down the hill to meet you." Makeebah says.

"I'm on my way." Aisha replies in a hesitant tone.

Abbottsford projects was a place she cared not to be. throughout Philly they're known as slimeville.

The bitches are raggedy and the niggas are trifling.

They would set up their mother and sell their own souls for an eight ball of coke and some alright tree. So enthusiastic Aisha couldn't find herself to be.

Makeebah, at all cost, wanted Aisha gone. She orchestrated a robbery that would leave Aisha dead.

In her plan Aisha would pull up to get her. And while they were on their way to Club Horizon Makeebah would get a phone call alerting her that the location had changed. And for them to come out Feltonville to Marquan's house.

Once there, Makeebah, Marquan and Tariq would rob and shoot Aisha, leaving an ounce or two at the scene of the crime to make it look like a drug deal gone bad.

With all the minor details worked out, this would be Makeebah chance to cut into Mujahid. She was looking to play the role of the bitch there for moral support in his time of need.

In her mind this would make her a sure shot for the affection of Mujahid.

As well as rid him of the bitch who put him away.

Just as Aisha hits 29th and Allegheny, still in traffic, stopped at a light, she calls Makeebah to let her know her whereabouts. Also to be at the bottom of the hill so she wouldn't have to wait.

As she was pulling up she didn't see Makeebah.

Ready to call her again Aisha grabs her phone.

Just as she was scrolling down her phone list for Makeebah's number, she sees her coming down the hill at the back of the projects.

"You slow as shit bitch!" Aisha said in a hostile tone.

"I seen one of my young jawns and she had the raps... My bad."

Makeebah replied.

As Aisha was about to hit the expressway, since it was a straight run back downtown to Center City, Makeebah phone rings.

Not trying to eavesdrop, but Aisha hears Makeebah's conversation in part.

Not fully aware of what was being said, she pulls over once she heard Makeebah ask, "What's the address?"

Aisha didn't want to get on the E-way if something had changed in the meeting. She didn't want to be forced to go out of her way.

Once Makeebah hangs up the phone, she says to Aisha, "We got to go to 2nd and Olney."

"For what?" Aisha asks.

"Marquan got stuck with his son, so he got to baby sit. He said he couldn't find nobody to watch him."

Looking forward to hittin Club Horizon, Aisha was disappointed. However, she never let on that she was.

It had been awhile since she been out. And wanted to hit the club scene.

But business is first priority. So she begins on her way to the destination Makeebah had told her to go to.

Once at 2nd and Olney, Makeebah directs her to turn left onto a little block named Mascher Street.

Then she says, "The address is 5642."

Just her luck it was a parking spot right in front of the house.

Now parked, Makeebah calls Marquan's phone and informs him that they were out front.

Aisha heard Makeebah say, "Come open the door."

As they began to get out of the car Aisha looked around noticing a white van with tinted windows.

It had been following her since she left her house.

At first she thought her mind was playing tricks on her.

There's white vans all over the city, so this had to be a different one, she thought to herself.

Then she noticed the unique license plate that read PLAYA!

Believing that the van following her was feds or kidnappers, she tells Makeebah to, "Hurry up!"

Then rushes into the house of Murquan.

"What's up cuz?" Marquan asked greeting Makeebah.

"That's Damon?... He got big as shit." Makeebah said grabbing for the baby.

Not interested in the family reunion, Aisha came to conduct business.

"Hello." Was said by Marquan in a wanna be seductive sexy voice extending his hand, looking to have it shook by Aisha.

As a lady does, she returns the greeting.

Also asks in a pleasant but firm tone, "Yall ready to conduct business?"

Now in full business woman mode she gets down to the purpose of the trip.

Marquan opens a duffle bag with stacks of money tied down with rubber bands, wrapped in thick plastic like phone books, and states, "As we agreed upon $112,500.00... Where's the product?"

Taking the duffle bag to the car, Aisha puts it in the trunk. And pulls out of the same trunk a Fendi oversized bag.

Looking up the block she sees who else but Unc.

She signals for him to come down the block.

As he's making his way down the block, she begins to walk towards him smiling.

She explains to him that he had her nervous thinking he was the feds, or niggas trying to get a bitch.

"Why you following me?" She asks.

"Once you told me about your business deal I decided to make sure you was cool. I didn't mean to make you feel uncomfortable, or be up on you like you couldn't handle your business." Unc said.

"I'm glad you did follow me... Come on in."

Unc jumps out the van and begins to follow Aisha into Marquan's house.

"Yo! Yo!... What's going on?" Marquan asks in a panicky voice.

"It's cool... This my husband's Uncle. He here to make sure business is done properly."

Then she hands Marquan the bag.

Unaware of the plan Makeebah had orchestrated, Aisha signals to Makeebah that she was ready to leave.

"You coming or staying?"

Makeebah gets up with a puzzled but disappointed look on her face. And begins to walk to the door with Unc and Aisha.

Pissed off that shit ain't go down as she had planned, Makeebah demands Aisha to take her back to her Aunt's house, where she had picked her up from.

Aisha drops Makeebah off and heads home to put the money up from her first big deal.

Then she was going to enjoy a night out on the town to celebrate.

24 BEGINNING OF THE END

Eighteen months in on a twenty-four month sentence imposed by the parole board, Mujahid begins to become bothered by the whispers that echoes through the streets and roars through the jail house yard.

Agitated and annoyed as well, Kay hated to witness how the gossip was eating Mujahid alive.

Being his walkie, Kay confronts Mujahid and informs him that there was a cat in the jail that had information he could use.

Upon walking to a corner of the yard where Mujahid had sectioned off as a place to offer the daily salats while indulging in the recreational period offered to the inmates, Kay signals to the young boy Molly to come over.

"What's up dog?" Molly asked as he approached Kay and Mujahid.

"So what's the 4-1-1 on the data you was spitting to me earlier?" Kay asks.

Molly begins to say, "Like I told you... my man was telling me about this chick from Philly, he was dicking her head off, named Aisha.

She getting to a dollar he said. Sis on some rugged shit. She gonna be the next to blow.

I don't know her, or even ever heard of her... But niggas on her top! She definitely trunk material."

"You say your man told you all this?" Mujahid asked.

"Yeah!" Molly replied anxiously as if he had just gotten a green sheet to make parole.

"Who your man?" Asked Mujahid in a demanding voice with a devilish smirk on his face.

"His name is Rico, but everybody calls him Poo-Poo. He from Chester, Highland Gardens projects.

He a good dude... Just can't leave them chicks alone.

They his only down fall.

Straight goon, but a sucker for love when it comes to those broads." Molly spits back.

"By the way, my name is Mu... And that's what I do... I take money! I need to get with your man and get some data on sis, so I can make something happen!

Trust when I tell you, you will be rewarded. And get what's coming to you for the data." Mujahid assured Molly.

"I'm on that! All I want is an outlet and connect to get on when I touch" Molly said before departing the cipher in which those three had formed.

Once Molly skated off, Kay begins to ask Mujahid, "What's that all about? You ain't gone really break that chump off is you?"

"Nizzaw, be easy, I got this under control...

But I am a man of my word, so he definitely gone get what's coming to him." Mujahid states with a look on his face that one could easily mistake for the face of the Grim Reaper.

As they're walking the yard a youngin approaches and shakes the hand of Mujahid. Then says, "What's up old head? You alright?... You know I got major love for you like you was my biological. When you gone let me put that work in and become a soldier for the family?"

To most, they had no clue as to who Mujahid was, or the things he had going on in the streets.

But for some reason he had taken a liking to this youngin by the name of Pee-wee.

A West Philly cat, 60th and Market original. He was a well groomed youngin with the potential to be a boss if ever given the opportunity again.

Pee-wee was serving a 100 year bid for five robberies.

Originally when he fell he only had a cop shooting and a homicide on top of a robbery. Somehow he came from underneath of the drama. But the D.A. was so pissed they couldn't book him solid with a life bid, they gave him four more robberies on top of the one he already had. Then gave him five 20-40 year sentences running consecutive.

To many this would have been considered the end of the line, But to Pee wee, he took it in stride and kept it moving. He refused to give up. So every chance he gets, he in the law library trying to give that time back.

Pee-wee a soldier whole heartedly. Niggas fear him like they did on the streets beyond the walls of the penitentiary.

He not no tough guy, or bully, but when you violate, he on your ass with the sentiments of Satan taking a new soul.

He had so much of a reputation within the jail they had nick named him two swords Pee-wee. Due to the fact he had two homemade knives that resembled swords.

And wasn't by far scared to use them.

Once he was sentenced his family turned their backs on him. So his mind frame is that of a loner.

He was deep down kind of glad they had shown their true colors.

They molded him without even trying.

His resentment towards them became his shield of armor.

Emotions was a weakness used by your enemy to manipulate and dictate your structure. Without any, nobody had anything to hold over his head.

Therefore, war meant war in his mind.

The average man works hard to protect his loved ones so that they wouldn't become a liability in times of war.

Pee-wee used that to his advantage.

Although he was booked, he still remained in contact and in control of his team of goons he had once ran with.

He formulated the plan, they executed it to perfection.

Mujahid use to walk and talk to him, keep him calm within the prison, so that he could and would stay out of solitare, or in jail terminology, the hole.

As time went on they began to form a bond. Almost like they were brothers, same mother same father, but with the understanding that business was business, Fuck emotions and love when it came to business.

Mujahid had further extracted the last little bit of veins in which emotions traveled. Yet, left Pee-wee with the complete understanding of self discipline.

"Your chance is coming soon to display your loyalty and honor for the family." Mujahid assured Pee-wee.

"Real talk?" Pee-wee asked with excitement and enthusiasm.

"Just give me a minute to put something together for you. But stay on board cause it's gone be major." Mujahid instructs him.

With that being said, Mujahid and Kay spun off from Pee-wee and met up with Hat, the third part of the trinity in which Mujahid had orchestrated behind the walls of the prison.

Hat was a silly type dude on the surface, but a hazardous to your health type fella to cross. A real rider who had proven himself time and time again to those who just wouldn't take heed to the warnings.

He was serving a 5-15 year bid for homicide. He was rather young compared to the type of caliber dudes Mujahid had normally surrounded himself with.

Hat had fell as a juvenile and managed to groom himself into a well rounded general, who had risen through the ranks within the prison walls.

Once all three parts of the trinity was together, it was no telling what was to erupt. To the outsiders looking in this was a sign of trouble.

Still walking the remainder of the yard period, the three of them chit chatted and conjured up a plot to silence the whispers. And allow the screams of their persons to be heard without being noticed, or even associated with the madness about to take place.

With the yard being terminated, all three men began to head for the housing units in which they were being housed on.

As time progressed, a week and a half to be exact, word and the information Mujahid had requested reached its destination. And manages to become music to his ears.

It seems Molly has become a viable and reliable source in obtaining this information. However, Mujahid didn't particularly care for him.

Loyalty was a major thing to Mujahid. Molly not once exercised an ounce of such.

If Rico was supposed to be his man, why was he shoveling his data to an outsider without even knowing the intentions of that person.

Not to mention he flat out talked too much.

Mujahid had seen his kind on numerous occasions, too eager to be known and liked, that they just rambled on about any and everything. Not realizing that those same loose lips would be the reasoning behind their departure from this world.

Now with the information within his grasp, Mujahid began to put his plot in effect.

The information couldn't of came at a better time, being as though Aisha was supposed to come visit on the same day the data was rendered.

Going about his normal routine in preparing for the visit, Mujahid was anxious to expose the data on the inside, but cool as a fan on the outside.

With a mind as vindictive as his, it was no telling what was to come, or how he'd react towards Aisha knowing how she went outside the realms of their prior agreement.

Mujahid wasn't strict when it came to the governing of her social life. He had given her clear instructions as to how to maintain and still remain within the realms of their relationship.

He had done time before. And knew what doing so entailed. He clearly gave Aisha the green light to do her.

Along with such instructions came special rules and conditions.

Mujahid understood that in the course of his physical absence came wants and needs that he knew would come about. So he explained to Aisha to just be neat and discreet. Your business is your business. Regardless of what, you still have a husband.

The bond they share should mean enough to her to protect the foundation in which they've structured their existence.

Since she knew it was very few people who didn't know who Mujahid was, she would have to play the surrounding states of New Jersey and Delaware. Also, all the little counties in Pennsylvania.

Secondly, she couldn't bring nobody, or none of her business to Mujahid's home.

If it was to go down, take it to a hotel, or the home of the chump she was dealing with.

Lastly, remain loyal and honest to the hand that feeds you. Take nothing out the circle to contribute to nothing, or nobody, but Mujahid.

All stipulations Aisha agreed to. And assured Mujahid that things would be handled delicately.

Now with her business being broadcasted only means she didn't value, or care enough about Mujahid, or their relationship, to conceal her actions. Therefore, in Mujahid's mind, she's to be used as she exposed her hand to be, a whore without any morals.

With the new outlook on their relationship it was no telling how Mujahid would handle the scenario.

Still grounded with his structured composure in tact, he awaits the call for him to report to the visiting room.

Just like clockwork the call comes at about noon for him to report to the dance floor.

Upon entering the visiting room Mujahid notices that Aisha had already been seated.

She had the normal dishes from the vending machines that he had always eaten.

Happy to see Mujahid, Aisha smiles and embraces him as usual. She begins to give him the low down on the current standings of his business, when abruptly Mujahid cuts her off.

"Fuck all that... Let's talk about you..." He says in a firm demanding tone.

"Me... What about me?" Aisha asked with a surprisingly shocked look on her face.

"Let's start with the structure of our agreement. It seems it's been a breach of security in that area..." Mujahid goes on to state.

Confused and dumbfounded, Aisha begins to question the whereabouts of such a topic had come from.

"Regardless of where it came from... It got back to me. And in detail." He confirms to her.

Then went on to say, "I gave you lead way to do you... And yet, you must of wanted me to know your business because discretion wasn't exercised.

So is it anything you want to say to me?" Mujahid asks.

"They lying... I haven't been doing nothing!... I swear!" She pleads.

Then begins to get dramatical with the tears and whispers.

Not wanting to cause a scene, Mujahid gives her assurance and contentment believing her obvious lies. And proceeds to continue the visit.

In his heart he felt as though the relationship had been abandoned. And the relations were to be immediately terminated soon as he touched the streets.

For now she can play the part of wifey. But the reality is, she was a stranger.

Next to no loyalty, a liar held next position on the list of things that was intolerable to him.

If you lie, you steal, which means you cheat, so trust couldn't be established or founded.

2.5 MAKIN IT HAPPEN

On his way back to the housing unit Mujahid comes across Pee-wee in the cut at the top of D-Block.

Unaware of the task he was about to be confronted with Pee-wee addresses his old head with open arms.

While embracing Mujahid Pee-wee asks, "What's the situation? I see you coming off the dance floor."

An obvious give away since Mujahid had been wearing his state boots.

Only time they're worn within the institution is for war and visits.

Mujahid was so laid back war wasn't even in the equation.

"Yeah, I rocked out a little bit, nothing major." Mujahid said with a serious look on his face.

"So what it do! Why you of all people stretching your hand on D-Block?

It gotta be major for you to grace the terror dome in person." Pee-wee asks.

Although D-Block was the initial block Mujahid had did his time on before making parole, he avoided the whole atmosphere of D-Block this time around.

He was only a parole violator, which meant, he was gone shine again.

On D-Block the mentality is so unrealistic Mujahid didn't want to risk the chances of catching a jailhouse case. So he stayed on B-Block. A unit designated for PV's.

"Like I told you, I have some work for you to handle." Mujahid replied.

"So what's the business?" Pee-wee asks excitedly.

"I need you to put your team on standby... This is a two part task." Mujahid told him.

Then Mujahid further goes into detail.

"First I need you to make that cat Molly disappear. He a snake. Before they get a chance to bite you, they have to be decapitated. So take care of that! And remember... Low profile, no heat, in and out."

"I'm on board. I know how to move in a cage full of vultures. So what's up with my team?" Pee-wee replies. And asks with a tone to be mistaken as confusion.

"One thing at a time Pee-wee. Just handle the front task and the rest gone come to you. Just be on point." Mujahid said smiling before walking away.

Although he smiled, the matter at hand was far from a joking matter.

Once Mujahid orchestrated a hit, the results always became ugly and gruesome.

The right hand of Mujahid was Kay. A midsized fella, medium build, a Southwest Philly renegade.

Mujahid had once said jokingly, that Kay was short for Kat, because Kay had to have at least nine lives. He was hit on several occasions and still here to tell the story.

He laid back and quiet, but secure enough in his actions that his presence causes chaos within the prison.

It's a known fact that if Kay pays you a visit, it ain't good. Thus far, there hasn't been anyone left behind to attest to the actual tactics he imposed.

He and Mujahid linked up on some humbug shit. Some cats from Pittsburgh tried their hand and decided to move out.

A mistake on their part.

Kay handle his business in the yard solo and Mujahid took a liking to how he moved.

Mujahid became the mediator and dead the matter before it got too far out of hand.

From that day on they've been inseparable.

Kay was going home within a matter of days.

Mujahid had to work fast in order to have all the players in position to execute his plan.

Kay was dealing with a chick by the name of Anisa who was going to school for Forensic Science.

All through his three and a half year bid they had become real close.

Their choices of conversation were always out of the ordinary.

Anisa was heavy into her schooling. She would always try to explain the basics to Kay.

Perhaps this was her way of incorporating her studies into her daily activities so she wouldn't forget what she'd learned, or studied.

By Mujahid being Kay's walkie they had no secrets. Kay would come back and tell Mujahid all the crazy scientific shit Anisa was doing.

One thing that really caught Mujahid's attention was, how Anisa had an assignment to alter or manipulate DNA.

Being street fellas this topic was far from what interest people of the streets minds. The end result was a head banger.

Anisa had extracted the original white cells out of a sample of blood and substituted them with white cells extracted from a follicle of hair.

Therefore, changing the DNA profile to fit that of another being.

Once Kay told this to Mujahid his mind began to race with all the possibilities of how he could eliminate Aisha without the bloodshed.

In order to do so Kay would have to cut into Rico to get close enough to get DNA.

It's been bothering Aisha how Mujahid could've found out about her affairs.

She did everything in her power to be discreet. And yet, word still managed to travel back to Mujahid.

Realizing that her carelessness is a major sin in the realms of Mujahid's world, Aisha's outlook and perspective on their relationship has also changed.

She knew how Mujahid's mind worked, or so she believed.

Somehow the vibe she was getting for the last few months didn't feel like us, it was more of a You and I competing, waiting to be debuted as the battle of the sexes.

Aisha knew that on a straight up all out war scale, she had no win against Mujahid.

The amount of soldiers that was prepared and ready to die for him was unreal.

She began to strategize to even the playing field.

She knew at some point it was either herself, or him. And life had just begun for her, so in her mind all that echoed was, I be damned if I allow my emotions for this nigga to cause me to be dropped and boxed in somebody's cemetery.

Aisha quickly began to gather her thoughts.

Within moments she was on her cell phone calling the team she put together, alerting them that an emergency meeting was in order.

First one she called was Makeebah. After about 3 or 4 rings she answers.

"Hello!" Was all she said.

"Where you at?" Aisha asked.

"I'm down the projects. why?" Makeebah questioned in an authentically baffled state.

"I need you to get the rest of the girls and meet me at my house ASAP.

We got some real shit to take care of... We got to get our shit together. And tight.

Be at my house by 7:30 tonight." Aisha instructed in a tone that immediately warranted attention.

Then she hung up and dialed another number. This time a male answers the phone.

"What's up baby girl?" Was the greeting this man offered.

"I need some assistance." Aisha replied.

"What's the problem?" He asks.

"I need some artillery. A lot and fast." She told him.

"Damn, what you done got yourself into?" He asked in an almost jokingly voice.

"That's irrelevant! I just need to know can you make it happen or not?" Was the words Aisha spoke in a serious tone.

"How soon you need them?" He asks.

"Now, if you got them." She replied.

"Dig this... Spin by my spot and grab what's on deck for now while I make a few calls to get you right." He told her.

"I'm on my way!"

Before he could even reply Aisha hung up.

Ready to start her mission, Aisha opens her safe and grabs five grand. So that it wouldn't be no issues or dilemmas as to the seriousness of her purchase.

Her mind was made up and there was no turning back now.

She leaves her house and immediately heads for the destination of her mystery man.

This meeting would be the last step in a process she's been secretly planning for a while now. Slowly but surely she has been preparing for the chaos about to take place.

She already had leased an apartment out in Delaware about six months prior. She bought a new car that she didn't drive in Philly, so it wouldn't be recognized.

Everything was done under the radar.

Only one who she informed and took with her, was her little sister Najah.

Najah had no clue that all this was hidden from Mujahid. She had taken a liking to him. In her eyes, she was none the wiser as to what was going on.

All she knew was Aisha set her up in a phat crib, copped her a car to drive, put her in a nice neighborhood.

Anything else she didn't feel a need to know.

Aisha was by far no dummy. The whole time Mujahid been away she was stacking her money and investing in all sorts of ventures to generate legal revenue. All this time she's been building a nice little nest egg to fall back on just in case Mujahid decided to cut her out the loop once he came home.

This little secret gave her an advantage over Mujahid. As long as he didn't know or suspect such, he wouldn't plan for the fall back, which would throw his whole plot off, due to miscalculation of the unknown. This was an added bonus she absorbed from watching and eavesdropping on Mujahid over the course of his run in the streets.

In her mind she figured, you would have to be a damn fool not to learn from a man with so much firsthand knowledge.

An hour into the ride Aisha finally arrives in a rather quiet section of the Greater Northeast Philadelphia.

After about 10 more minutes of driving she pulls up to a house that looked like something out of a white woman's picket white fence fantasy.

Once she parked, she calls this mystery man back.

"Yizzo!" He answers.

"I'm out front." Aisha states.

He makes his way over to his front bay window and peeks out.

And then said, "Pull into the garage."

Still watching to be sure she wasn't being tailed until she gets in the garage, out of a door that one could only assume leads into the kitchen, comes a dude that by first look you would only conclude he was a Jamaican, carrying two brief cases.

He gets into Aisha's car.

"This is what I got on deck for now." He states.

Then proceeds to open the brief cases one by one.

Aisha's eyes became as big as fifty cent pieces. And a smile as big as the sun broadcasted across her face.

"That's what the fuck I'm talking about." Was all she could say.

The man goes on to explain to her what she was getting.

In the first case was a Calico with a fifty shot clip. And under it set in foam, was a Tech nine with a thirty-two shot clip.

In the second case was two chrome .380's.

The glare from the chrome made them more appealing to her.

There was also a .25 caliber and five clips. Two nine shot clips for the .25. And three eleven shot clips for the .380's.

Without a word being spoken, he had known Aisha wanted what she seen.

"How much?" She asks anxiously.

"For you since we already do business, just deduct the cost from my next flip on the re-up." He said.

As anxious as she was, he could have asked for fifty grand and got it.

Quickly Aisha agrees to the deal on table.

"As soon as the rest come in I'll hit your phone and arrange delivery." He goes on to say.

Then exits the car once Aisha nods to confirm they're in agreeance.

Aisha backs out of the garage and gets on her way.

Not even bothering to conceal the cases. She left them in the front seat on the passenger side as if they was her special guest on her journey.

2.6 THE MEETING

6:50 pm, Aisha notices it's almost time for her to meet the girls.

In the course of her running errands during the day she had completely lost track of time.

She wraps up the last of her errands and heads home to meet the girls.

Upon arrival at her house she notices that Sidney was already there.

Sidney is her assassin.

It's kind of hard to imagine somebody as pretty as her could be such a stone cold killer.

That's how most niggas get caught up.

They get so far into the fantasy of what they gone do to her, that they forget their place and come out their comfort zone. Leaving their lanes wide open.

She uses that to her advantage. That's what makes her so damn good at what she does.

Sidney is a 5'5-1/4",165 pounds, redbone. Her dimples makes her even more sexier. Her body was crazy, with an exquisite exotic look.

She had hazel eyes. And under the right light they sometimes look gray.

Soft spoken with a smile to die for, pigeon toed and stand so far back on her legs that at times it resembles a horse's stand.

Also, a perfect shaped ass like a heart.

Her measurements is 38c-22-40.

God must of short changed somebody for her to come out looking so good.

Aisha gets out and greets Sidney.

"Hey Sid..." Aisha says in a manner that almost suggest they haven't seen one another in quite some time.

"Bitch! This better be good! I'm supposed to be at black house right now." She replies sarcastically.

The tone in her voice already told the story to Aisha. Therefore, automatically once she said black, Aisha knew it had to be about dick.

Black wasn't her dude. He was a nigga who was married to the streets. He was so caught up and out there that he had no time for relationships.

However, his fuck game was so delightful that Sidney would actually schedule days in advance, for months at a time. If he could bottle that shit up and sell it, he would be Oprah Winfrey rich within a year's time.

"Be easy, he ain't gone nowhere." Aisha said to her in an aggravated tone.

"You know he will... He ain't got no problem moving on to the next bitch. And ain't no telling when the next time he gone be free." Was the remarks Sidney shot back at her.

As Aisha was opening the front door of her house she hears a shout out, turns and sees Rabbit, just as loud as she could be.

Rabbit was the total opposite of Sidney in all aspects, far as personality and styles of execution.

She was brown skin, braces, more on the wild side. 5'2", 154 pounds, alright when it came to looks. She wasn't ugly, but it wasn't nothing sexy about her at all. Her body was of a deformed build. But she was so thorough it was impossible not to like her.

Her measurements were 48DD-25-38. From the front her hips gave the illusion that she had a fat ass. Once she turned around she looked like the average white girl.

"Hey Rabbit." Aisha responded in a jolly tone.

"So you don't see me bitch?" Sidney said in a sarcastic manner to Rabbit.

"I forgot your evil ass was gone be here." Rabbit sarcastically replied back.

"Don't start, she missed her appointment with black to be here." Aisha informed Rabbit.

"Oh shit! This must be some major shit going down!" Rabbit said in a startled yet intrigued tone.

By the time the women could get all the way in the house

Makeebah and Neek comes strolling down the block. And mingled into the mesh of women as they all entered the house.

While Aisha set up the brief cases on the dining room table the women engaged in idle gossip, catching up on the latest of events to occur to one another.

Although all these ladies were killers in their own rights, they still were females. So of course all the antics that normally occurs when women group up still happened.

Everybody talking at one time, yet everybody's conversation was still heard and understood by everybody.

"Listen up ladies..." Was the sound that caught the attention of all the women and brought silence to the group as Aisha spoke.

"...Over these last 22 months we been holding shit down and doing us.

All the small shit in between was a field test to prepare us for this moment.

The plate we been eating from is being threatened. And as a unit we got to get really dirty and come up out this shit.

Mujahid said, we had to extinguish the flames up under his team. In order to get the dues we deserve... We have to get rid of the family. And it has to be from the blindside.

Yet done to perfection, cause once we draw blood, ain't no turning back.

Therefore, we got to perform like it's our last stand.

Don't look at the team, look at the task.

And then execute the task.

First order of business is to dismantle the foot soldiers. I'll take care of that.

I just need yall to play the middle and get rid of the council… from the top all the way down.

I even got some toys to get us started."

Once Aisha opens the cases all the whispering and gossiping commences again.

This time more so on the choices of weapons.

Everybody grabbed a gun except Neek. She the only one who didn't play with them.

Her weapon of choice was a straight razor. She'd rather slice your throat than shoot you. She was terrified of guns. Because of this fear she always had to get intimate, up close and personal to perform her magic.

Don't let her fear of guns confuse you, she was the most vicious of all. She was like a surgeon with a straight razor.

Aisha goes on to get into details as to how the attack would take place.

The meeting lasted longer than expected.

By the time everybody was on board and on the same page, time had flown, it was close to 3 a.m.

Once everybody left to prepare for the battle ahead of them,

Aisha sat in her living room holding her .380, her new found love, within her arms.

Gazing out the window in deep mediated thought is how she enjoyed the nakedness of the wee hours.

She wasn't playing and meant business, so a clear head was definitely in order.

She knew they had to bring the family down within sixty days. That was all that was left before Mujahid came home.

So time wasn't of the essence, nor was it a good friend of hers.

Last night was a real wake up for Aisha. It seems the life she never dreamed of has made a way to plague her perception of life.

This time two years ago, she was content going to her 9 to 5 on a daily basis, struggling to make ends meet.

Now she ignore those days and live as if she was destined to be who she's become.

Staring in the mirror not recognizing the image that's looking back at her, Aisha begins to brush her teeth and prepare for the deed she etched in stone to be done.

Once her morning ritual is complete, she grabs her .380 and puts it in her coach bag.

No sense in prolonging the inevitable is what echoed in her head.

Unc was still in control of the family daily operations. He managed to keep things in tact as Mujahid had left them, so far so good.

Yet still, Unc felt a void within his soul. As a whole, he really couldn't complain about his life. What was surrendered in his early was made up for in his later years.

He really wanted Mujahid by his side. He wanted him to see the progress he's made since having the ball dropped in his lap.

Yesterday's gone, so all Unc can do is keep it moving until Mujahid returns.

As part of his weekly ritual Unc called Aisha.

"What's up? Heard from Mujahid lately?"

"I went and seen him last week. I'll be back up there Thursday." Aisha assured him.

"Anything you want me to tell him?"

"Yeah, let him still know I'm on top of the game... Running shit like he would if he was here. If he need something let me know!"

With that being said, He and Aisha hung up.

Moments later after his phone begins to vibrate. He answers it and a voice on the other end informs him that Shaq was killed.

"What happened!" Is all he said in a puzzled upset tone.

He listens to the details of the murder then hangs up to call Hafiz.

"As Salaamu Alaikum Unc..." Was the salutation offered.

Being side tracked by the noise he was hearing in the background

Unc responds, "Wa Laikum Salaam... Where you at?"

"Out and about. Why, what's up?"

"You heard about Shaq?" Unc asks.

"Naw"

"He got killed this morning, Bilal went pass his house to grab him, and when he got there Shaq was laying in the bed butt naked, handcuffed with his throat slit from ear to ear." Unc said.

"I'm on my way down the block, meet me there!" Hafiz demanded of Unc.

Unfolding and being shaped in a whole new direction, Unc's day had just began.

Once he gets to the block Unc sees everybody conducting business as usual. Not understanding why nobody is riled up to strike back on the person, or persons responsible for Shaq's death.

He gets out his car and makes his way to Akbar's house.

While on his way, a young boy stops him and questions him as to how many he wanted, referring to the narcotics that was being sold on the block.

Ignoring the youngin, Unc continues to make his way to Akbar's house.

Normally Unc would of spazzed on the youngin, but Unc knew that not too many foot soldiers knew who he was. He was more happier that they wasn't letting nobody get by unscathed. They were on they job as they should be.

Unc never played the block, so for him to make an appearance only meant something had to be wrong.

Just as he was about to knock on the door of Akbar's, the door opens and Abdul Maalik was on his way out.

Last time something like this happened they ran down on the previous owner of the block they were pumping on.

Nervous and scared, Abdul Maalik automatically says to Unc, "Akbar not here. He stopped pass earlier, but he got a phone call and rolled out.

He told me to hold the block down until he got back."

Absorbing the information given to him by Abdul Maalik, Unc about faces and proceeds to the next block over to the house they used as a safe haven to hold work in.

This was the house where all deliveries and transactions went down in. In order to see the inside you had to be a council member, or doing business with one.

As he made his way down the block, his phone rings once again.

He answers.

This time it was Hafiz calling him back.

"I see your car where you at?"

"I'm on Rush street on my way to the spot." Unc replies.

Then the phone goes dead. As he checks to see if his phone died, along side him pulls up Hafiz.

"As Salaamu Alaikum..." Hafiz offers.

"Wa Laikum Salaam..." Unc replies.

"What's the situation on Shaq?" Hafiz asks.

"I really don't know... All I can say is Bilal called me and told me how he found him." Unc replies.

Then proceeds to render the following comments, "It just don't sit right with me... The way he was found goes outside his character.

Plus, he don't take nobody where he lay his head at..."

Hafiz interrupts him before he could say another word and says,

"Don't worry, the wash ain't done! We just got to see who comes out in the rinse.

Until then, put it out there that it's a cash reward for any information about the situation.

Keep heavy tabs on the idle talk, cause one thing for sure, the streets talk worse than a bitch.

We just got to get it before the police get wind.

Best believe when the streets whisper they got their ears to winds to hear the echos."

Gazing off with a hazy look in his eyes, Unc just sends back a simple head nod.

Then says, "True that."

Ready to get back to his prior affairs, Hafiz prepares to exit the conference offering only salutations as he leaves, "As Salaamu Alaikum!!!"

Meanwhile, more nervous and jittery than ever, Aisha began to feel the pressures of her task.

Her mind was already made up, Mujahid has to go. That's the only way she will ever feel safe.

As long as he's alive the results of her actions will always haunt her.

As she conducts business as usual, she began to hear the all too eager whispers of the streets.

It seems the reward Unc offered is being threatened to be collected.

Although no names have surfaced as of yet, she feels it's her obligation to clean up any loose and sloppy work rendered by her team.

So far, only thing that can be said is Shaq left Flavaz, his favorite club, with a female with a fat ass.

As always with men, a fat ass and pretty smile will side track the business at hand. It's like they on a quest to fuck every ass that wiggles loosely.

Mujahid had always told her that the key to war is not the muscle or manpower, but the art of seduction. Discipline is the key factor.

As well as the fact she had a team of loyal bitches that was willing to sacrifice their pussies to score an advantage.

Knowing this, she devised a way that would clean up the loose ends that she had lingering around, as well as take down the family.

About a week later she pushed her first pawn to set her plan into motion.

She called Unc to get the ball rolling.

She made up this elaborate story of how word got back to her that this dude from Chester named Rico had Shaq set up and killed.

She played her part to the fullest.

99

She provided names, addresses and phone numbers to get in touch with Rico.

It seems she wanted to get rid of Rico before Mujahid came home. Although, Mujahid had always told her to keep her business neat and discreet, she wasn't sure how that tender dick nigga was gone act once Mujahid came home.

It was already evident he was caught up. He'd already violated the first rule of their affair, keep their business their business.

It got back to Mujahid.

She knew she ain't tell nobody, so it had to been his nut ass.

It's crazy how the thoroughest of dudes become the lamest of all nuts once a little pussy juice run down the shaft of their dick, she thought to herself.

The next day Unc began to spread the newly discovered data to Hafiz.

"You sure about this Unc?" Hafiz inquires.

"It's definitely official from a reliable source." Unc assures him.

"How reliable is your source?" Hafiz questions.

"Look I'll put my life on it... If they say this is how it went down... Then that's how it went down!" Unc replies with surety.

"Then it is what it is!" Hafiz spews back before giving the salutations as he rolls out.

With the data Unc had given him Hafiz begins to make the necessary calls to properly take care of business.

Within minutes he has a squad saddled up and riding out Chester to get at this Rico cat.

Upon arrival at the destination that Unc assured him Rico would be at, Hafiz calls the number given to him.

It rang for a brief minute before somebody answered.

"Hello..." The voice on the other end says.

"Can I speak to Rico?" Hafiz asks.

"Speaking!... Who this?" Rico replies.

"Naw fam it ain't that type of party... Relax... be easy, I'm just trying to do some B.I. with you." Hafiz states in a tone that almost demands immediate attention.

"You still ain't say who it is! Nor what type business you trying to do!" Rico reminds him.

"Not on the phone... Meet me some where we can talk face to face. Best believe it's a helluva come up." Hafiz tells him.

Allowing his greed to overtake his better judgement, Rico sets up a meeting at the Howard Johnsons Hotel across the highway.

"I'll be there in about a half." He assures.

No intentions on actually making the meeting, Hafiz hangs up.

That was just a ruse to get the cat out his house.

About fifteen minutes later a tall slender dude exits the house Hafiz and his team had been watching.

Just as he makes his way to a 98 Bonnie sitting on deuces with a custom paint job, a car pulls up beside him and boxes him in.

Within seconds it sounded like the fourth of July on that quiet little block they were on.

You could hear the screams of AK's, SK's, Riot pumps and the roar of the 41 magnum Red Hawk that Hafiz toted.

What appeared to be a nice block to raise kids on in the cut, had suddenly became the epitome of what it was to live in Iraq during the war.

Slumped over in the driver side of the pretty ass Bonnie was the target they had intended to hit.

The sound of sirens alerted the team of killers it was time to retreat back to Philly.

The next day while watching the channel six news Aisha hears the incident being broadcasted. They had referred to it as a page out the O.K. Corral chronicles.

With a smile on her face she turns the volume up and further listens to the details of what the media is referring to as a drug deal gone bad.

With only a dutch and eight ball found, the media making it out to be botched up robbery attempt.

Regardless of what the media making it out to be, Aisha was feeling content that the pawn she had just sacrificed opens the lane for her to capture a bishop and knight.

Now with Rico out of the picture, it was time to push her next piece to further get her to the point of check mating Mujahid.

She calls up Sidney and informed her it was time for her to step up to the plate and bat.

Unaware that Sidney had already been at the plate, all she was waiting for was the pitch.

Sidney had elected to play Hafiz close since he was already so fond of her.

For the last few weeks she's been boo loving, opening him right on up.

In fact, she had been with him the morning Unc called and told him about Shaq.

She had been occupying Hafiz's time so that Neek was able to get a clean spill on Shaq.

With the next move already in motion, Aisha begins to work overtime.

The clock has never been her friend. All that's left is thirty days until Mujahid is back in play.

2.7 BUSINESS NEVER PERSONAL

Sidney began her day just as normal as any other day. The only difference was she had a date with destiny. It was her job to eliminate Hafiz. She had spent enough time him to get a feel for his character. She had known it wasn't gone be as easy as all the other killings that she had done. Hafiz wasn't no slouch, nor was he laid back enough to just let her off him.

In fact, the only time he was vulnerable enough to strike against, was in his home. She had to get up close and personal. A task that was gone be harder than it sounded.

Hafiz didn't allow too many people to get close to him. Yet alone, invite you to his home.

If she intended to get into the safe haven he had formed, then she was gone have to go beyond the call of duty.

She knew she had him open. All the quality time they spent together was all in preparation leading up to this moment.

In the beginning, she was just teasing him with little grinds and feels. Then she acted like she was drunk and he took advantage of her drunkenness.

Well aware of the incident, and fully functional, she had played her hand just as she did to give him a taste of her head game.

She wasn't no amateur so she knew he would want more. Eventually it progressed into a business venture.

What nigga was shelling out nickels for the feel of her warm mouth. It had gotten to the point he wanted a taste every night. So before he took it down for the night he'd call for his regular.

Of course she played the unwilling participant.

She had explained to him that she wasn't feeling going home afterwards all horny and wet. So Hafiz started peeling off a stack and a half for a half and half shot.

For Sidney it was cool. She was able to get her shit off every time. Due to the fact he was in a chair, she had to do all the work.

She rode him like a bucking horse, while letting the muscles in the pussy contract.

Hafiz was hooked.

The only problem was all the events took place at her crib and not his.

She tried to get him to let her spend the night, but Hafiz wasn't going for it.

He was real arrogant and cocky.

He felt like because he had money, he looked down on everybody else. Nobody was worthy of his personal space.

The only way to invade his personal space was to treat him to something he'd normally wouldn't get.

Knowing this, Sidney calls Hafiz.

"As Salaamu Alaikum..." She offered.

"Wa Laikum Salaam..." He returned.

"What you trying to do tonight?" She asks seductively.

"Depends on what you trying to do!" He said.

"I'm not gone fake it, I'm feeling your shot. Had I'd known it was gone be all like that, I would of been put my claim on you."

Hafiz laughs and threw back, "Well what's stopping you now?"

"Stop playing... You ain't got no time for me."

"I always got time for you... Every time you call I drop everything and squeeze you in... You definitely my lil' buddy."

"So if you feeling me like you saying, why you ain't never invite me to the king's lair?" She asks jokingly.

"My door always open for you." He claims to her.

"So tonight we can go the extra mile? It's only right you mark your territory." She throws at him.

"So what you saying?" He asks confused.

"Open me up all the way... No holes barred." She says in a voice so sexy, Hafiz wants to cum immediately off the sound of her voice alone.

"My back door been closed for a minute, I wanna be freaked tonight." She adds.

"I got you! What time you trying to get together?" He asks.

"Let me finish up my errands and I'm a call when I'm ready. You gone come get me, or do I got to come to you?"

"Just call me and I'm a come scoop you." He tells her.

"I'm a hit you A.S.A.P... As Salaam Wa Laikum."

"Wa Laikum Salaam."

Now in position to infiltrate the fortress, Sidney prepares for this date with fate.

She had really wanted to get her ass loosened up, so this was killing two birds with one stone.

Coughing up a storm from the mega pulls she was toking from the Sour Diesel dutch she had been smoking, Rabbit feels her phone vibrating.

She looks down at the screen.

It read one new text message. She opens the message and begins to read.

The text said: get ur mind right... time 2 c ur work in action.

She just smiles and sends back: HA! HA! HA! BITCH!

Then she goes upstairs and gets a box out the back bedroom's closet.

Leaving the box unopened until she finishes her dutch.

Once done she opens the box and pulls out a chrome .45 caliber pistol with hollow point bullets.

And then begins to screw on a silencer.

She kisses the gun and says out loud, "I been waiting to see you in action baby." Referring to her mega toy.

Because of her so pleasant, happy go lucky nonchalant attitude towards life, it was almost hard to see Rabbit in the light of a killer.

Nonetheless, she had a job to do.

And best believe it was gone get done.

Regardless of who, or what stood in her way.

Unable to drive, Rabbit calls a cab to get her to her destination.

While waiting she rolls up another dutch.

Then sits on the door steps of her house and blow solo to the head.

Once the cab arrives, she gets in and tells the driver to take her to 11th and Cumberland.

Normally the ride is a pleasant journey for her to lay back and sight see to.

For some reason it seemed to be extremely long this day. Not sure if it was the anticipation of using her toy, or traffic was just that backed up. Whatever the reason was, her patience began to thin.

Finally arriving at her destination, she pays the fare and proceeds to go into the 2543 high rise building of the Fairhill projects.

She got on the elevator and went to the 10th floor.

As the doors open to exit she sees her cousin Nakeisha.

"Where you going?" Rabbit inquires.

"I got to go to work." Nakeisha responds.

"I was on my way to your house." Rabbit informs her.

"Here goes the keys... Make sure you here to let me in at exactly 2 O'clock." She said before handing Rabbit the keys.

Then adds, "If you do leave... Bring my keys to the job so I can get in."

Since she only worked across the street from the projects at the Dew Drop bar, it shouldn't be no problem to get the keys back to her.

Once inside the apartment, Rabbit sits her oversized purse on the table and begins to make a few calls from her prepaid cell phone.

Finally she calls Unc.

"Hello." He answers in a nonchalant tone.

"Unc, I need some onions for the steak I'm cooking..." She says figuring he'd put it together that she was placing an order for some work.

"Who this?" He asks inquisitively.

"It's me... Rabbit."

"Who phone you on?" Unc asks not recognizing the number.

"This my work phone." She replied.

"Where you at?"

"I'm down the projects." She answers.

"You want me to get sautéed, or whole onions?" He asks to understand the nature of the transaction.

He'd already known she wanted a point due to the lingo spoken.

In the drug game, the key is lingo. Had she said a definite number then the amount would have varied.

She said, some onions, meaning four.

Since the bird is chipped up in sections, she would have to take the half to keep shit straight.

"I want'em whole so I can season them myself." Rabbit states.

"Soon as I get in range I'm a holla." He says to let her know he's on his way.

Then hung up.

To herself she thought, why Unc?... But business is business, so the thought quickly faded out of her mind.

She angles her position on the balcony of the apartment she was in to get a clean shot at her target.

45 minutes to an hour later, she gets a call from Unc to let her know he was in reach.

She informs him to meet her on the 15th floor.

Not wanting to use the balcony for the long distance shot, because it was kids in the park playing, she decided to play indoors.

As she makes her way to the 15th floor, she notices it was some fiends in the exits getting high.

She couldn't risk blowing the deal, so she meets Unc at the elevator.

Soon as the doors open, she let off two shots that hit him in the chest.

Still moving, gasping for air, she stands over top of him and let two more go into the cavity of his cranium.

Then makes her way to the exit and unloads four shots to the head of each fiend in the exit.

Nothing personal, but they had seen her face and could identify her once an investigation was launched.

She walks down the exit on the opposite side of the building until she reaches the 10th floor.

Then she goes back into the apartment in which she came and dismantles her toy. And begins to puff her dutch.

Once again pulling out her phone, she texts a message and sends it to Aisha's phone.

The message read: 2 nite was a great nite.

Then grabs her belongings and made her way out the building.

Looking forward to the festivities that was to take place this evening, Sidney really put herself together to entertain, as well as be entertained.

Every since Black first dickmatized her, she wasn't able to enjoy, nor benefit from the relations of others. So this was her chance to get her shit off again.

Even if it meant she had to work a little harder to achieve the pleasures she wanted to feel, she was prepared to do so.

Not really sure if it was the motion in the ocean, or the ship that sailed, that made her quiver. One thing she did know was, she aimed to answer the age old question pondered.

In her freakishly seductive mind she had been comparing and dissecting the pros and cons of the evening she had arranged.

She thought to herself, Black wasn't as big as Hafiz, but Hafiz couldn't twerk it like Black either.

Hafiz tongue was one of gold.

Black ain't eat pussy.

Black wasn't into foreplay.

Hafiz was definitely into stimulating the mind before unifying the physical with the mental.

Even in darkness the evening still promised mystique.

Sidney had been out shopping all day to look her best.

She brought a lace bra and thong panty set to highlight the curves that she knew all men wanted.

It was something about a fat ass swallowing up a G-string that drove men wild.

For most, the sight alone had them ready to buss.

The bra was half cut. It allowed the nipples to be seen. Her areola was extremely brown. And bigger than a fifty cent piece. So even if she wanted to she couldn't hide them.

She even had the garters that connected the fishnet stockings to the thong.

Her only dilemma had been the color. She wasn't sure if she wanted red to create the ambience of passion, or white to captivate the innocence of a young inexperienced girl.

When men perceived you as innocent, they tend to try to put more into the experience so that perhaps if nothing, you come out the experience saying, he definitely put hip, back and shoulder into it.

Since Hafiz had been paralyzed she decided to go with the color black. This created the allure of freedom. As well as, made the statement, if your heart not strong don't even engage.

She had gotten a stick of lip gloss that made her lips speak without a word being said.

Her hair had been done in a pinned up bun with just a lock of hair streaming down, curving to the contours of her pretty face.

Not too fond of such, she even goes as far as to get a nice pair of stilettos to compliment the attire, by which was only covered up with a light spring trench coat.

She looks in a full length mirror before closing the coat to be sure everything is in place and tempting enough to make Hafiz want to wife her.

With the approvals of her own taste, she makes the call to Hafiz.

Upon arrival, Hafiz couldn't believe the details of this LiL' dick eater he'd become so fond of.

He had never seen Sidney in the light in which she was to be examined this evening.

Thinking to himself, damn this bitch bad!

With only a look, she could tell Hafiz was enjoying the vision of beauty before him. She knew he was staring. So as she made her way around the car to enter, she begins to walk slowly. Yet, allowing her hips to twinkle hard enough to illustrate the wiggle and jiggle her ass had done so well.

Although it had been hidden under the coat, Hafiz could tell it was poppin.

At a loss of words, he doesn't speak the whole ride to his crib.

Even when spoken to, he just smiled and nodded to accommodate the void of words.

Sidney just sat there smiling.

And a beautiful smile it had been. Noticing the excitement in Hafiz's loins through the bulge that wouldn't stop throbbing in his pants.

After about a half an hour of silence, with the exception of the music playing, they arrive at their destination.

It had been a big beautiful home from the outside.

It really did look wholesome and serene. She could understand why he'd never brought no one to his home.

The average bitch from the hood wouldn't, or couldn't appreciate the serenity offered by being where she was that evening.

Once inside, she damn near fainted at how plush he had it laid out.

Italian marble floors, high arched ceilings, solid gold trimmings. And an elevator that went from the first floor to his bedroom.

The fish tank that sat in the wall at the foot of his bed was beautiful. It had to have been at least, fifteen feet long. And four and a half feet wide, with the most exotic and exquisite fish she had ever seen.

Now realizing that, it wasn't he looked down on the less fortunate, but understood they couldn't be appreciative of his taste for the finer things in life humbly.

Still in awe at the sight she was seeing, Sidney pulls it together and focused on the man in front of her.

A totally different man she was witnessing behind closed doors, as opposed to the one who she had met and known.

Hafiz slides out his chair and onto the bed. He breaks his undeclared vow of silence with a few chosen words.

"I know you ain't come to stare at my fish tank."

A smile lit up her face that radiated enough energy to burn out the sun.

She drops her bag onto the floor.

And soon afterwards, following the pattern, her coat ends up there as well.

With nothing but the outfit and heels that she had brought earlier to shield her nakedness, Hafiz signals for her to come to him.

Slowly walking and taking the longer route, so he could see how scrumptious her ass swallowed the thong she had been wearing.

Stopping to adjust the strap on her shoe so he could get a up close and personal view of the thong disappearing into the cushions he had wanted to penetrate so badly.

Finally making her way over to the bed, she climbs on and straddles Hafiz like he was gone break a bucking filly.

Taking the initiative to undress him, applying wet warm kisses to the areas unveiled, all the way down to the waistline.

Allowing her tongue to lead the way to heavenly adventures, She stops to suck her own breast while gently rubbing her wet fingers though the depths of her pussy.

Feeling like she had to get the first nut off manually to enjoy the eruption of the next, she lets out a moan and flings her head back with her eyes closed tightly.

Hafiz grabs her breast and begins to fondle and pinch her nipples.

Once he felt the tremors of her thighs against his side, Leaving her space to fall back with the free hand to brace herself for whatever was to come.

Just like the wailing of a siren she lets out a scream so loud that it startles Hafiz.

Jerking and twitching like she was in a deep ritualistic trance.

Once done, Hafiz questioned "Was it good for you?"

She just smiled and proceeded to undress the lower half of his body.

This time allowing her tongue to trace up and down, along the shaft of his manhood, until slowly she arrived at his balls. And begins to sensually devour the massive treats she had been massaging.

Feeling the throbbing of his shaft, she works her way back up it. Not stopping to open her mouth. It all happened so fast. And before Hafiz knew it he was deep within her throat, unloading what felt like gallons of jism into the warm wet canal that had engulfed every inch of his manhood.

Thinking to herself, that was just a warm up.

She had known that he had taken a viagra.

She spins around without coming up for air, until her pussy is mounted on his mouth. That was what she wanted most of all, to get her pussy sucked unbelievably.

Hafiz obliged the thought. He began to allow his tongue to tease her pussy.

Tracing the lips inside and out, until finally letting the wetness of his tongue manipulate and massage the clitoris.

Feeling the eruption about to burst, she begins to grind his face like she was slow dancing in a house party pinned to the wall.

Letting out a slight moan as Hafiz inserts a finger into her ass at the same time.

Feeling the tremors coming on again, Hafiz begins to insert multiple fingers into her ass as she's cumming simultaneously.

Increasing the depths and speed until her body goes limp.

The slightest of touches causes Sidney to go into spasms.

Ready for some dick, she mounts his manhood trying to capture every inch.

She thrusts while gyrating, wanting to feel him in her stomach if it was possible.

Once she orgasms again, she slides off the dick and jams it in her ass almost in a manner to identify with being raped.

Rocking back and forth, fatigued with determination to take advantage of the opportunity awarded to her.

She wasn't gone allow that viagra to be wasted.

She was gone get as much out of it as possible.

For the next couple of hours, she done what she aimed to do, get her shit off whole heartedly.

Awakening from a slumber that had been induced by the activities the night before, Sidney slides out the bed and goes into the bathroom, grabbing her bag and coat as she enters.

After cleaning herself up she comes back out into the bedroom and without emotion, or recollection of the events that took place last night, she just cold-bloodedly empties three shots into Hafiz. Two in his head and one in his heart.

Looking at her task as just business, she leaves the residence and finds her way back to the realms of the city of Philadelphia.

Once in her crib she turns on the bath water to soak off the juices of Hafiz. Then texts Aisha with a smiley face confirming her job has been done.

2.8 SNAKES IN THE GRASS

Not understanding why, or how the news of the street always managed to surface on the prison circuit so fast. It seems that before either body was cold Unc, or Hafiz, the word had spread through the prisons.

Feeling angered, depressed and vengeful, Mujahid hibernates in his den, refusing to leave his lair in which he dwelled.

Saddened by the news of losing not only his team, but his family as well. Although he and Hafiz had their differences, they still shared one factor that held them together as adhesive does, they were of the same bloodline.

Not realizing the significance of the bond until a speck has been spilled.

Even though he had come to grips with the reality that the life they chose would only end up in one of two places; jail, or the grave yard, he still pained to actually have his brother and uncle buried.

While sulking in the sorrow of the losses, Mujahid hears his name announced for a visit.

Believing it was Aisha coming to console him, he takes his time preparing for the visit.

When he finally made his way to the visiting room, he was shocked to see who had been there waiting on him.

Confused and curious as to what she wanted, he makes his way over to her and asked "What's the situation?" In a modest tone.

Happy to finally get a chance to be in the graces of her object of affection, Makeebah asks, "Damn no love!... It's cool!... I'm sorry for what happened to Shaq, Unc and Hafiz..."

Feeling saddened by the mention of the incidents, Mujahid just put his head down and closes his eyes in attempts to shut down the flood gates before they overflow.

Then she goes on to offer, "I tried to stop the move, but it was too late."

Raising his head in a state of shock, as well as disbelief, he asks, "What the fuck you talking about?"

In an innocent and naive tone she begins to explain to him how Aisha had orchestrated the hits.

At a loss for words, he manages to get out the question, "Why?"

Makeebah takes a long breath then goes on to say, "She used them to weaken your line of defense.

Her ultimate plan is to bury you...

The money is going to her head.

She think she the last American mafia princess out there."

Not really surprised, more so assured of his notions that Aisha had changed, went through his mind.

He then shoots back to Makeebah, "So why you telling me this?

You the one who supposed to get next to me?"

"Come on Mujahid, we bigger than that. We been rockin heavy since before forever...

I'm telling you cause I'm your homie."

Wanting to just pour her heart out and let him know she was in love with him.

Instead she keeps her composure and continues.

"I don't want to see you come home and become a victim of circumstances. You a good dude!

Plus, my big homie!

So I can't see, or let it go down like that.

I'm fucked up you would even allow such a thought to entertain you like that...

You one dude I could never see myself crossing, you him! And for him I would bolt down and take a few... Real talk!

I'm putting myself in the line of fire just coming up here to let you know what's going on." She says with uncertainty as to whether he would put her out there, or not.

Just sitting in silence, baffled, allowing the information he had just gotten to soak in.

He finally breaks the silence and asks, "Who had the audacity to carry out a hit of this magnitude?

Everybody knew they was my folks."

"She used the chicks from crosstown to do it... Sidney, Rabbit and Neek." She says with a certain conviction as to assure him he knew who she was talking about.

"You mean 9th and york...

The bitches that used to do hits for the zoo Boyz?" He asks with a touch of disbelief that they were even able to infiltrate the structure he had built.

"Yup that's them... Aisha made them part of her team." She says confirming their identity.

Not saying a word, only staring off into twilight land, rubbing the hairs in his beard in a motion as to lay them down over and over again.

Makeebah then asks," So what now?... What do you need me to do to keep you safe?... You want me to earth her? For you, I'd definitely rock out, just say the word."

Hoping that Majahid would assign such a task to her.

But he just sat there staring into space as if he was pondering the request.

Then abruptly let's out, "Naw... Just go on as normal... I'm not gone let her know you been to see me... And you don't tell nobody you been here. I mean nobody! I'll be out there real soon. I got you!

Just keep shit like it is... And keep me in your visions."

With that being said, they began to buss it up about the news and daily functions of Aisha.

Mujahid picked Makeebah's brain so thoroughly that he knew her thoughts before she did.

"Visits are terminated." Was the warning to alert the visitors that the visiting room was closing.

Makeebah exits, feeling good about her deed.

She believed she made an indentation in getting a step closer to having Mujahid see her in a different light.

Perhaps, one that would fulfill her dream of belonging to him exclusively.

Anxious to get back to general population, Mujahid exits the visiting room with only one thing on his mind, he knew he had to kill Aisha. He didn't want nobody to do it. He wanted to do it personally. He wanted the satisfaction of standing over her looking into her eyes and seeing the fear, as well as terror that would emerge.

He wanted to let her know she could never do, or outsmart the cat that made her.

Within a matter of time the streets heated up fast. The once whispers were now roars.

With the family wounded Aisha's demand became much larger.

The profits were doubling but the risk of survival was increasing at a rate three times the profit margin.

No longer under the umbrella of the family, Aisha began to feel the effects of her actions.

It seems all the low lives, peasants, fleas and crabs had surfaced in no time.

She had become the talk of the city.

Apparently, she had achieved her dreams of becoming the boss of the city.

She now realizes that Unc was a major part in her success. Without the muscle, the vultures will circle she's learning.

Her team was about their work, but the fact they was females made them more likely to be tested. She knew the test would soon come.

And being defeated was something she couldn't fathom.

Aisha came across this dude named Dawud. He was from out West Philly.

A midlevel dealer, but anxious to grow.

He just needed a line that could handle his demand. As well as eat with him, as opposed to off him.

Aisha had been in the Dog House, a hood breakfast shop on Germantown and Lehigh, it's a networking cafe.

If a nigga wanna get on, this was the place to meet a line that could make it happen.

Dawud cut into her.

The confidence he asserted demanded that Aisha notice, as well as listen to him.

He made her an offer for protection and loyalty, in exchange for work at a discount price.

He made her familiar with his status out West Philly. Plus, assured her that the up and coming team of goons he had affiliated himself with was stand up and dedicated cats.

The offer proposed seemed to be reasonable. The muscle he had backing him was very much needed at the moment.

However, what she didn't know was that Dawud was the

little brother of Mujahid's youngin Pee-Wee. He was sent to cut into her by Pee-Wee, per Mujahid's orders.

Failing to realize that a man of Mujahid's caliber, is and always will be, respected. Therefore, any and everybody is dying to prove their allegiance to him. They content just being in the graces of his presence.

In her mind she had it all planned out to use Dawud and his team as muscle to combat Mujahid.

Also keep the streets in pocket.

In reality, she had just agreed to expose her hand without even knowing it.

She introduced Dawud and his team to her team. Everybody was cool with it. And a new family had been born. So she believed.

For the next couple of Weeks shit was poppin. The word had spread that Dawud and his team was up under Aisha to take care of any problems that may erupt.

Her blocks were back in order. She had managed to collect a few new ones.

The roars again became whispers.

She was on top of the world. Feeling herself like she never felt herself before. She was ballin out of control.

She had copped new wheels for everybody.

She was making arrangements to take the whole squad to Vegas.

She furnished everybody with jewelry and a new wardrobe.

She was throwing away money like it was confetti at a New Year's celebration.

She was definitely feeling herself.

Until one day she receives a call alerting her that turmoil had arisen.

Sidney had been killed.

Her body was found in a vacant lot down South Philly.

She had been shot in the face several times. Her throat had been slit. Her body was mutilated and set on fire. 70% of the flesh had been burned off the bone.

Whoever was responsible made sure it was a closed casket funeral once she was found.

Aisha felt a certain type of way, due to the fact, Sidney had been one of her top lieutenants.

Her ace in the hole for when niggas under estimated the volatile nature of the female.

Loyal to the core, no rap. If it needed to be done Sid was on board.

Aisha tried to create a panic in the streets. She had offered a $50,000.00 reward for the information leading to the identity and whereabouts of the person, or persons responsible for the death of her lieutenant.

The streets wasn't talking. Nor was the whispers echoing.

Whoever done this really knew how to secure their work, She thought to herself.

This had been the beginning of the end for Aisha. And she didn't even realize it.

One by one her team was falling like dominoes.

Neek had been found decapitated.

Her head was the only thing recovered. The rest of her body had been missing. Almost like it had vanished into thin air.

Rabbit had been dismantled, with the pieces mailed to her mother.

Every other day a new piece was received until the body had been fully recovered, with the exception of her heart out her chest.

Whoever had been on Aisha's ass had been getting closer to their target. And she knew it. So she kept herself surrounded by Dawud and his team at all times.

In her quest to secure herself, she didn't realize that her immediate loved ones were also within the radars of vultures.

Although she had lived in Delaware, she had transported Najah and Naseem to school in Philly on a daily basis.

Never once entertaining the thought that they also were prey.

Until one day she receives a phone call demanding a million dollars for the return of Najah.

In a hysterical panic she scrambles to see if indeed the kidnapping was real or not.

She calls Najah's phone. It just rang and went to voice mail.

Concerned as to where Naseem was, she tracks him down at school.

She immediately picks him up.

In a hysterical state she asks, "Where's Najah?"

Without hesitation from fear of the tone in Ashia's voice, Naseem responds, "She went to see her boyfriend."

"Who her boyfriend?" Aisha asks hoping to at least get a name to point her in the direction of where to begin to track down her sister.

With only a shrug of his shoulder as an answer indicating he didn't know, Naseem continues to look scared and nervous.

Najah had told him not to tell nobody she had ditched school to go see her boyfriend.

Not knowing, or understanding the extent of her actions, Naseem feels like he did something wrong.

A few moments later Aisha gets another call from the same blocked number as earlier.

As she answers, she can hear the cries of her sister.

In a begging frantic toned voice, she asks the questions, "Who is this?

Why are you doing this?

What do you want?"

Then adds, "She a kid... She don't have nothing to do with nothing!

Please don't hurt her!"

"Don't worry bitch! Long as you do as I say, she'll be returned unharmed." The voice on the other end of the phone states.

"What do you want?" Aisha asks.

"I want a million dollars... just as I told you earlier...

I want it delivered in large bills.

I'll call you back with the details of the drop off...

And remember, no cops, no tricks, or she won't see the darkness of tonight come.

I'll call you back at exactly 3:30 to give you the details. So you have until then to come up with the bread." The voice says with the conviction of being serious.

Immediately Aisha drops Naseem off at her mother's house.

Prior to doing so, she called Dawud and told him to meet her at the block she was in route too.

She also informed him to bring a few of his goons heavily armed.

Just in case an attempt was to be made on her baby's life, she was gone be ready and prepared.

Their sole purpose was to guard the block her mother's house was on, she thought to herself.

"So what's up Aisha?" Dawud asks with concern in his voice.

"My sister was kidnapped this morning." She said.

"You serious..." Dawud shoots back in a surprised yet worried voice.

"What's the ransom?"

Knowing that it was gone be something heavy cause of the type money she was getting.

"They want a mill..." she says.

"You got that type of money laying around?" He asks.

"Trust and believe I got access to it...

Thats a drop in the bucket for me to get my sister back." She assured Dawud.

"So what's the move? How you wanna handle this?" Dawud inquired.

"Fall back, let me handle this! Just make sure my baby safe." She said before peeling off to get that bread together for the next call.

She quickly arrives at an apartment building in center city.

Then proceeded to hurry into the building.

It seems this was a stash spot that the family had used to keep the drama to a minimum.

They knew that all the ruckus wasn't gonna go down in Center City.

Those white folks were on their jobs. If anything suspicious, or didn't look like it belonged, they were calling the law guaranteed.

She had been there enough times that the doorman knew who she was and buzzed her in on sight.

"Hello Mrs. Aisha." The doorman offered

"Hi Mark." Aisha responds.

Noticing the look of disgust on Aisha's face, he further asks,

"Is there something wrong?"

"No, just tired and ready to get some peace." She replies back to him not wanting to alert him that a situation had occurred, nor that they kept the type of money she had to get in the apartment.

Once in the apartment she heads straight to the kitchen and empties out the deep freezer.

To the average person it would appear that the freezer was packed with food.

To those that knew had known that in the center of the freezer was a wooden box, filled with the profit and booty of the business, she had worked so hard to control.

She takes out ten ziplock bags filled with hundreds counted out in hundred thousand dollar stacks.

She packs the freezer back up.

Places the plastic bags filled with money into a duffle bag that she had went and got out the master bedroom's closet. Then sat and waited for the call she had anticipated.

She still had a half hour or so to spare before the deadline of her call, so she calls Dawud to check on the block.

She was a little relieved that everything is alright according to the news Dawud had given her.

Still on edge waiting for her call.

Her phone rings at 3:20 according to her clock on the kitchen wall.

Without waiting for it to ring a second time she answers. "Hello."

"You got the bread?" The voice on the other end asks.

"I got it." She replies.

"Good, now bring it to Kensington and Lehigh..." The man instructed her.

"No cops baby girl, or this thing gone get ugly." He also adds.

Without delay Aisha hangs up and makes her way to the destination she was instructed to be at.

Once there she gets another call telling her to take Lehigh to Aramingo Avenue.

In route to the second location, she gets another call telling her to make a left on Aramingo and take it until he tells her to stop.

Then the phone goes dead.

Thinking she disconnected it, she began to panic.

After riding for about ten minutes, she gets another call.

This time the call instructs her to make a left on Venango and a sharp right into the mini mall behind the Wendy's.

As instructed she does so.

She parks in front of the Dairy Queen and waits for further instructions.

This time when the phone rang the voice told her to get out the car and walk to the Dollar store.

As she begins to get out she grabs for the duffle bag, but the voice on the other end of the phone instructed her to leave the black bag in the car.

Shocked at how he knew the bag was black.

Then realizing, whoever it is, has been following her the whole time.

She leaves the bag and goes into the store.

She's then instructed to go to aisle four to the deep freezer at the back.

She proceeds as instructed.

Then the voice tells her to meet him on Broad and Lehigh at the train station.

In her mind, she was getting frustrated and wanted to cuss this pussy out, but she can't chance anything happening to Najah.

As she gets back into her car, she notices the bag is gone.

She begins to freak out.

Then suddenly remembers she was being watched.

So whoever was watching her must have took it.

Wanting her phone to ring one last time to confirm the money was received, she goes to Broad and Lehigh.

After driving for twenty minutes, or better, she pulls into the train station at Broad and Lehigh.

Not seeing anything, not even a car in the parking lot, she pulls in and waits for the next set of instructions.

After about ten minutes, she gets the call she had been hoping for.

"Hello..." She answers in a frustrated, yet docile tone.

The voice responds with, "The money was ten grand short."

Knowing it was an accurate count, she just apologizes and offers to compensate the ten grand with another twenty grand.

Then the voice tells her, "The package you looking for is in the train station at the R7's waiting booth." And abruptly hangs up.

She rushes to the R7's waiting area.

She notices Najah sitting on a bench with her back turned to her.

She calls out to her sister, but she didn't respond.

Believing that the incoming train was harboring the sounds of her voice, she makes her way to Najah.

Just as she reaches out to embrace her little sister she sees her throat had been slit.

Falling over from the touch Aisha had given her.

Aisha falls to the ground herself screaming, asking for an ambulance, begging for someone to hear her screams.

She had been the only person in sight.

The sounds of the incoming train had silenced the screams she allowed to roar from deep within her soul.

She sat there on her knees rocking back and forth, holding the lifeless body of her little sister, while offering nothing but tears to comfort her.

2.9 PAIN IN HER EYES

The loss of her sister saddened Aisha. At the same time shredded the last bit of emotions that her soul was capable of possessing.

Heartless and without emotions, she took to the street like a renegade, ruling with an iron fist.

The areas she didn't control, she sent her goons to get.

Regardless of who, or what, she was determined to make the city pay for her loss.

After engaging in a brief meeting with her team to inform them of their next plan of attack, she was suddenly approached by a young lady of no significance.

To the average person this lady looked to be homely. A real nerd. Someone you would picture to be into all the scientific affairs. A pretty face, by far an ugly duckling.

With the right baller in her life to polish the rough edges of the diamond, she definitely could be a hot girl!

In a humble, yet submissive tone, this lady calls out to Aisha.

"Excuse me miss... Miss... Miss..."

The softness of her voice made it difficult to hear her yells.

Pointing to herself and looking around to be certain this lady was talking to her, Aisha responds in a hostile tone, "What's up!... You know me!"

"I don't actually know you, but I do know of you...

You're Aisha right?" This woman asked with certainty in her voice and admiration in her actions.

After a nod assuring her she had been talking to Aisha, the woman goes on to ask, "Is there somewhere we can talk? I really believe you need to hear the details of what I have to say."

Aisha stares at the woman with a look of puzzlement, as well as, curiosity. Then leads the woman into a quaint little coffee shop on the corner of the avenue they had been on.

"You want something to eat?" Asked Aisha.

The woman responds with a polite "No thank you."

"How about something to drink?"

Again she responds, this time with a shaking of her head indicating the same no thank you.

After ordering a big boy special and a hot tea, Aisha asks, "So what's on your mind?... How do you know me?... And what can I do for you?"

"Actually, I'm a get back to the last question at the end of our conversation.

In the meantime, I'm a begin with a proper introduction.

My name is Anisa. I'm a student of the University of Penn." She says with a sense of proudness that alerts Aisha she was happy to be able to pursue her dreams.

Then goes on to add, "My boyfriend was Keith, but the people he dealt with in the streets call him Kay..."

Cutting Anisa off in her quest to speak, Aisha responds to the statement just made with a frank, "I don't know no Kay... or Keith."

"You do know a Mujahid right?" The woman asks.

Hearing Mujahid's name automatically caught Aisha's attention.

Without saying another word, she just nods to assure Anisa she had known Mujahid.

Then Anisa continued, "Keith just came home a little while ago. He was locked up with Mujahid.

He put me in an awkward position...

He came to me a few weeks ago and wanted me to set you up."

Shocked at what Anisa had just said, Aisha instantly looks around to be sure she wasn't being ambushed.

Then asks in a hostile tone, "What the fuck you talking about?"

Anisa explains.

"I'm a biology major majoring in forensics. We've been experimenting with DNA profiles.

I had explained this whole process to Keith awhile back.

He came to me and asked to transfer the DNA from a follicle of your hair into blood that the DNA had already been extracted from.

I inquired as to why he had been so adamant about having this done.

He didn't want to tell me, but he finally broke down and told me that Mujahid wanted to set you up to take the fall for a murder."

Anisa concludes.

Shocked at what she had just heard, Aisha takes a deep breath and begins to ask questions like crazy.

"What murder?"

"I don't know that." Anisa responds.

"How did you get my hair?" Aisha asks in awe.

"Mujahid had a C.O. get it at one of the searches when you visited him... That's what I was told." Anisa says with a tone that reflected her innocence.

"What do your boyfriend have to do with this?" Aisha asks confused.

"He was supposed to do the deed and set you up." Anisa responds.

And lastly, "Why are you telling me this?"

"Like I told you, I'm a student at the University of Penn... I'm not working, so the expenses tight.

I was barely making it with the help of Keith.

He suddenly came into a large sum of money and decided, he didn't want to be with me no longer, so he left me in debt."

Before she could get rest out, Aisha cut her off and asks, "How much money you talking?"

"Let's just say he don't have to work ever again in life." Anisa answers.

"Where did he get it from?"

"I can't answer that... I wasn't even supposed to know. It just so happened I let him borrow my car. And when he returned, I went to get a few things for school out of the trunk and discovered a duffle bag filled with money in plastic bags.

I asked him about it, he got mad and accused me of spying on him and left.

A couple days later, he returns my car and decided there was no longer an us." She says with a hurtful look of a woman scorn in her eyes.

Then proceeds to finish her prior statement.

"I'm struggling... I was hoping this information would perhaps be of value to you.

If not, is it something I can do to get on board to get enough money to pay for schooling?" She asks with desperation in her voice.

Before answering, Aisha gazes off into space, feeling like she had to step her game up now knowing that Mujahid was on top of his game.

She definitely could use Anisa.

She was unsure of how she could incorporate Anisa's talents into her master plan without leaving loose ends.

Coming back to the moment, Aisha answers Anisa with, "Don't worry you gone finish school."

Then she signals for the check for her meal.

And she and Anisa exits the coffee shop.

Later that evening, pulling up to an apartment building on the lower side of West Philly's University City, Aisha phones Anisa and alerts her that she was there.

Anisa comes out with an envelope containing a wad of cash and a brush.

Aisha then says to Anisa, "Remember what I said... Don't say nothing to nobody."

Then pulls off.

Anisa had made Aisha out to be some sort of super woman. The idea that a female could cause a scare into the city's most notorious males was alluring to her. This was a bitch she was destined to be close to.

Once Aisha pulls off, she calls Dawud and tells him she on her way to him, meet her at 60th and Arch.

Arriving at her destination she notices a commotion had been going on.

Some chicken head hood rats had been fighting over dick that didn't belong to neither one of them.

Paying it no attention, she falls back and waits for Dawud to get there.

Staring at the picture of Kay, saying to herself, I know this cat from somewhere, was all she could think.

Dawud pulls up and hops out a truck and into the Benz of Aisha.

"Whats going on over there?" Referring to the large crowd surrounding the commotion.

"Some stupid bitches fighting over dick." She replies.

Then shows the photo to Dawud.

"You know him?" She asks.

"Nah ma... who is he? Am I supposed to know him?" He shoots back to her.

"He somebody of interest to me... I want him found, but not killed. Just bring him to me." She demands.

After a brief pause of silence, she goes on to add, "The one who delivers him to me gets a bonus, 2 bricks of soft and a half of hard... Oils! On top of the Twenty grand already in play..."

It was a standing rule that any person of interest was an automatic Twenty grand to the one capable of getting him.

To her this was an incentive to keep her goons working hard.

"...I'm a make some copies and spread them around, so tell the fellas that everybody is in play." She finishes up with.

Normally she would pick the person, or persons, according to how she wanted things handled.

This time, all was fair, as long as he wasn't killed.

She tells Dawud to squash the beef between the chicken heads.

"They drawing too much attention to the block."

The next evening Aisha gets a call from Khalil.

He was a goon of Hafiz's that she had taken a liking to. He was a young boy, but about his work. He was a dedicated and loyal soldier. If he was a little older, he would have most definitely been somebody to tuck in the cut on the creep tip.

He was only 17. She felt she couldn't do babies. However, she did admire his determination to be a boss one day.

"Hello." Aisha answers.

"What's up boss lady... I found the dude you were looking for." He tells her.

"Finding him wasn't the issue, getting him to me was the job." She replied in a sarcastic tone.

Then continues on "If you can't handle that, I'll send somebody to you that can make it happen." Aisha tells him in that same Sarcastic tone

"Nah, I got it." He responds back to her in an almost heated tone.

He had hated when she talked to him like a sucker. She was the boss, he thought to himself.

But he would love to put two in her wig for G.P.

Aisha goes to the Family's counsel house on Rush street.

Then calls Khalil back and tells him "To bring him here."

She spreads plastic over the basement floor. Then places a chair on top of the plastic.

Meanwhile, on the part of Khalil, he was doing what he does. And that's earning money.

He calls Kay and lets him know that the line he asked him to get had showed through.

He also informs him that they would have to meet him down Jewtown.

Kay agrees. And prepares to get in route to the appointment he had wanted.

Khalil had met Kay on the humbug.

Kay cut into him asking to do business with him.

The type work he needed, Khalil couldn't handle. He had to get back to him.

Confused and not understanding the logic of Kay, Khalil only questions the intelligence of Kay.

The whole objective of the game is to come up.

It's only a stepping stone to do other things.

Yet, Kay had come up and now want to get in the game.

Not giving it too much thought, Khalil blew him off until Aisha started circulating the picture.

Then he became a check for him.

Khalil took this cat as a gift dropped in his lap.

Once at their destination, Khalil walks into the house, followed by Kay.

Soon as the door closed, Kahlil turns to face Kay and brandishes a chrome .45 caliber gun into his face.

He tells Kay to "lay on the floor."

Scared out his mind, Kay begins to try to talk his way out of the situation he found his way into.

"Yo!... You ain't got to do this!... I'm worth more to you alive than dead!

Please don't kill me!... I got a daughter to raise." He states in a scared whimpering whiny tone.

"Shut the fuck up and lay on your stomach." Khalil instructs and demands of the scared shitless coward crying to him.

In his mind he felt disgust that a nigga who profess to be ride or die, move out, G type dude, had resorted to the antics expected of an 8year old girl.

Had it been him, he had it made up in his head that he was going out in a blaze of glory.

For those that live by the sword, eventually gone die by the sword.

It's a thought that ever trigger-man has pondered at least once in their lives.

They had come up with a million and one scenarios of how to deal with it.

Although, it's rather difficult to speculate as to how one would act in a situation like this, Khalil had his mind made up, he was going out like a real G. He'd rather die on his feet than live on his knees.

Hearing all the whimpering of Kay, Aisha comes upstairs from the basement.

She couldn't help but to tremble at the sight of the man who had killed her sister.

Not out of fear, but from the overwhelming undeniable urges she had of finally playing god to this creep.

The day had come that she could actually avenge the death of Najah.

Not able to control herself, she kicks Kay in the face with her stilettos.

Then spits on him and ask, "You know who I am?"

Not wanting to admit he had known who she was, he denies knowing her. And states frantically, "It's a mistake... I don't have a problem with you, or nobody else.

It's not me. Please... Don't kill me!"

Aisha smiles and say, "I hope that million dollars was worth it... Cause it's damn sure gone be worth what I have in store for you."

Khalil had never seen Aisha out of character before.

He was shocked at the horrors that could be read through her eyes.

He thought to himself, I would hate to be the one to cross this crazy bitch!

Aisha demands Khalil to, "Take that piece of shit to the basement."

While Kay was being escorted to the basement, Aisha was in the kitchen gathering up a hatchet and carving knife.

Khalil handcuffed Kay to the chair that sat in the middle of the basement.

In his mind he felt sorry for Kay.

He had just wanted to collect his bread and be out. But the state of mind Aisha was in made it difficult to do so.

Listening for the footsteps when she stormed the basement, Kay is pleading for his life until Khalil gags his mouth with an old dirty piece of cloth found beneath the steps.

Aisha comes to the basement with the evilness of the devil in her eyes.

She immediately stabs Kay in the upper thigh like a slayer would do a stake through the heart of a vampire.

This was the first act of commitment to what she planned to show Kay. She wasn't playing, nor had intentions on exercising patience.

She stands behind him and places her carving knife under his throat and began to say to him, "Before we get started... I don't want no bullshit, or you will die!

I want answers. And I want them quickly.

Think it's a game and you lose pieces of your body... Now let's begin."

Before she asks the first question she tells Khalil to go put the big crab pot on the stove with some cooking oil in it.

Once he leaves, the questions began.

"So what Mujahid got in store for me?"

"I don't know Mujahid." He responds.

Without saying a word, she uses her hatchet and chop the first two toes off his foot.

"We not gone play these games." She reminded him.

"Now again, what do Mujahid have in store for me?"

Still screaming from the removal of his toes he doesn't answer.

Aisha draws back her hatchet and he begins to talk.

"Wait! Wait! He wanted you to be set up to teach you a lesson about calling cops."

"What murder was I supposed to bite?" She ask.

"Some cat named Rico."

Shocked at what Kay just said, Aisha asks, "Why Rico?"

"He was spreading yall business around. And that made him mad." He says crying and pleading for some type of relief and medical attention.

"What did my sister have to do with it?"

"I don't know your sister." He swears to Aisha.

She begins to carve sections out his face.

She calls for Khalil to bring that pot down with the hot cooking oil.

She strips Kay naked and pours it over his head. Watching the grease peel the layers of his skin off.

Screaming for dear life, Kay begs for a minute to explain, but Aisha was done talking.

All her words were gone be actions.

She uses her carving knife and slices of the genitals of this already tortured man.

He begins to shake like he was going into seizures.

Before he could pass out, she slit his throat from ear to ear.

Then begins to cut up his body into little pieces.

She was making it easy to transport the remains.

Once done, her and Khalil bags up the pieces and drops them off in the dumpster at a nearby construction site.

Feeling no satisfaction from the deed she had just done, Aisha begins to hate Mujahid even more.

She held him responsible for Najah's death.

Had he not involved Kay into the mix, Najah would still be alive.

His day will soon be here.

And when it does, I'm a take pleasure in seeing him die at the hands of me, she thought to herself.

Then went on to the next order of business.

PART THREE

AN EMPIRE CRUMBLED

3.1 CHANGING POSITION

Makeebah... What's up with you?" Aisha asks.

Being taken by surprise, not understanding what was meant by the question, Makeebah answers, "Nothing, I been trying to get things in order."

Not able to see Aisha's facial expressions to associate a vibe, or emotion with the tone in her voice, "Hold on my other line is clicking." Maheebah tells Aisha.

Although her other line hadn't been clicking. She just needed some time to get her composure intact to be able to vibe with Aisha to keep her in the dark about her visit to Mujahid.

"Aisha?" Makeebah says in an uncertain toned voice as to whether she was still holding on.

"Yeah, I'm here." Aisha replies.

And then goes on to add, "Damn, I ain't sleep with you last night...

I know you fucked up about our girls, but we got to shake it off and keep moving forward.

A lot has happened in these last few weeks. As my right hand, I needed to have you there... And you weren't.

You having second thoughts about this life we chose?...

If so, let me know.

This is not the time to have you cracking up on me...

So what's it gone be?"

"Naw, I'm still on board... I was just grieving.

I was gone call you today and see how you've been?

The weight really falling upon your shoulders, especially, the whole Najah incident." Makeebah says.

"I'm good! I mean my heart gone always cry for her, but I got to keep it together for Naseem." Aisha says with a tone of

145

anguish seeping through the breaths that left her body as she spoke.

"You a strong bitch!... I wouldn't be able to do it...

That close to home! you better than me." Makeebah says with a sense of respect for the way she's dealt with the death of her sister.

"So what you doing today?" Aisha asks in a voice that totally transferred over to the roars of her normal rotten self.

"Nothing... What you got planned?" Makeebah inquires.

"The normal activities... We got to get this money!

It don't stop to mourn the losses... It keep going on for days." Aisha says in a joking voice.

In her mind, Makeebah thought to herself, bitch your days is really numbered... I'm a be the one to spit on your grave when the casket drops.

Then goes on to comment on the statement Aisha made.

"I hear that." In a jolly tone like they was in a comedy club.

"What time you coming out?" Aisha asks.

"Soon as I get up... I'm a call you to see where you at."

"Make sure you call!" Aisha responds in a tone that said, I miss you.

The phone goes dead.

Both women hung up.

Aisha anticipating the call back from her right hand.

Makeebah dreading the moment she has to look in Aisha's face.

Filled with all the hatred in the world, Makeebah makes a call to an associate that she only dealt with when grime was involved.

"What it is my nig?" She greets her associate with.

"Damn, what's poppin... Ain't heard from you in a minute.

You must got something on deck for me today?" The man sends back to her, hoping that this was a business call as opposed to a what's up? how you doing? type call.

"It's me baby... You know I got you!" She responds back to the man.

After a light chuckle she adds to the mix, "Just meet me at 5 o'clock. And bring Roscoe and Bern.

"Roscoe was a .38 caliber revolver that had put in enough work to retire.

Bern was a .40 caliber that only roared a couple times.

Whenever Makeebah told him to bring both pieces, only meant it was some nice paper involved.

Without even questioning the sting, he just agrees and hangs up.

But before he hung up, Makeebah gave him the details of where to be at and what was to be expected.

Later on that day, Aisha had been with Anisa when Makeebah called.

Since Makeebah been missing in action, Anisa been filling that void.

Feeling elated that her partner in crime had been back in the picture, she jumps up ignoring the fact Anisa had been sucking her pussy.

"So I don't get to get my shit off?" Anisa asks feeling cheated that her turn to cum didn't look likely to happen.

"I got something nice for you... Just be easy mommy cat." Aisha says with a twinkle in her voice.

The sound of her words sounded so appealing to Anisa.

The curiosity alone was tantalizing enough to make it worth the wait.

Aisha gets up and goes into the bathroom and wipes herself off.

She dresses and leaves to go get Makeebah.

Excited to be in the company of her homie, she stops off to get a bottle of Grey Goose to celebrate the moment. Then makes her way to Makeebah.

Aisha had a smile on her face that one would believe she was happier than a faggot in boys town.

She has a glow about herself that's hard to ignore.

"What's up with you?" Makeebah asks with curiosity in her voice as to why Aisha had been cheesing.

"I got something nice for you... Or rather us." Aisha assures her.

"What is it?" Makeebah inquires.

Not wanting to be surprised, she wanted to know what she was walking into.

"It's a Marissa affair." Aisha says.

Marissa had been an innocent spanish chick that was confused in life as to her sexuality.

That was until she had a night out with Aisha and Makeebah, that cleared up all the confusion and also left her turned out.

She was good people.

Until she got caught up in that snorting phase.

Then the fun had ended. And the lifestyle swallowed her up whole.

"So who is it?" Makeebah asks not wanting to be caught up in a Marissa all over again.

Even though she got caught up in that circle, Makeebah was feeling Marissa.

It broke her heart to see a good girl as lost as she was.

"She tight work... Just like you like them... A redbone with all the qualities you admire, she nice!!!" Aisha says assuring Makeebah that this woman would be exclusively to her liking.

Not another word was spoken.

Only visions entertained the minds of the woman as to what was in store.

Pulling up to Anisa's building, Aisha phones ahead to let her know they had been back and was ready to party.

Anisa came to the door in her bath robe.

Hiding behind the door until the ladies was in, then revealing herself in the light.

"Anisa this Makeebah..."

"Makeebah this is Anisa." Aisha said introducing the ladies to one another.

"Hi." Anisa says in a shy tone.

"Oh, you a shy one." Makeebah said in an aggressive tone that lead Anisa to believe that she was a butch.

Not to mention the attire that Makeebah had been wearing, a polo shirt, baggy jeans, sagging with boxers coming out and some Jordans.

She wore her hat to the side cocked with a doo rag underneath. And strolled in a manner that screamed, I'm the man.

"Crack this." Aisha said giving Anisa the bottle of Grey Goose.

As they walked to the kitchen to get glasses, Makeebah reaches out and peaks beneath the robe of Anisa.

Liking what she saw, she smiles.

The ladies began drinking and conversing to get comfortable with one another.

Out of the blue Aisha asks, "You ready for the surprise I had for you Anisa?"

Not responding verbally, just a smile to say yes, Anisa let her eyes do the talking.

Before long, Aisha and Anisa had been naked.

Aisha straddled Anisa face.

Makeebah buried her mouth on Anisa's pussy.

These ladies were partaking in activities that would be difficult to visualize had one not been there to see it.

Aisha had managed to end up on the bottom.

Flat on her back and Anisa was doing her right.

Makeebah lifts Anisa's ass into the air. Then unzips her pants.

A long rubbery dick falls out.

Anisa was under the impression she was gone get some more that marvelous tongue to her pussy.

instead, she feels the contractions of her pussy muscles being stretched to maximum exposure.

Unable to speak, Anisa lets out a moan from the pleasure being administered.

By the end of the session Makeebah had fucked her in every position possible.

And got her strap on sucked.

Overall, it had ended up being a very nice day.

Aisha receives a call.

She gets up and prepares to leave.

"What's up Aisha?" Makeebah asks.

"I got to handle something, I'll be right back." Aisha said in a confident tone alerting the woman that whatever she had to do was gone be a piece of cake.

"You want me to rock out with you?" Makeebah offers.

"It's cool... You just chill and enjoy the treat." Aisha offers back referring to the delectable treats of Anisa.

Prior to getting to her destination, Aisha made a stop.

She goes into an apartment up north.

She comes out with a Bloomingdale's carry bag that she puts into the trunk and peeled off to her pre-arranged meeting.

She drove for about twenty minutes and ended up in Roxborough.

She makes a call prior to getting to her destination to alert her business client that she had arrived.

Just as she opens the trunk to retrieve the contents of the bag, she had placed there, she was ambushed.

Two men ran up on her, and without even speaking, just let off shots.

Aisha was hit in the abdomen and shoulder.

She falls to the ground and plays dead.

The men grab the bag and take off through a path along the side of the parking lot she had been in.

Believing that her time had come, she passes out.

By the time she awakens, she's in a hospital.

Her memory had been foggy, but her recollection of events was quickly coming back.

She had remembered that she had to meet her weed connect.

She also recalls hearing one man's voice saying over and over, "That bitch dead!" in her head, like a broken record.

"You up?" The nurse asks.

Shaking her head in a hazy daze to indicate she had been coherent, she begins to speak, "Where am I?" She ask in confused lost state.

"You're at Temple's Trauma Unit." The nurse responds.

Then goes on to add, "You're very lucky to be alive. Another centimeter and you would be resting with angels."

Not realizing that the woman who's life had just been spared was so rotten and deceiving that gates of heaven would open with fire sending her straight to hell.

Aisha then asks, "How long have I been here?"

"Since the 22nd at about 6:40 pm."

"What's today's date?"

"The 26th." The nurse answers.

Just as Aisha was about to get up and leave Makeebah comes in.

"So you made it back to our side." She says in a tone that sounded unsure whether she'd be back amongst them, meaning the living.

Then continues to ask, "What happened?"

"I got shot!" Aisha said in a joking manner.

"This serious Aisha." Makeebah responds back to the statement.

"I was supposed to meet the cat I was getting the tree from.

We had it set up as usual, same routine.

And out of nowhere shots just rang out.

The next thing I know, I'm here." She gives as her recollection of events leading to her hospitalization.

"Your connect called Anisa to let her know what was going on.

She was the last out going call you made besides him.

He said he found you in the parking lot dying.

He called the ambulance."

Wanting to know how much Aisha had really knew, Makeebah continues to grill her until she's sure she had no solid leads to what happened.

"Get some rest... I'll be back tomorrow to check on you." Makeebah says before leaving.

The next day Anisa had been the first one to visit Aisha.

Waking from a night's slumber with a headache, Aisha sees her there.

"What's up Anisa?"

"How you feeling?" Anisa inquires.

"I'm good just a little sore." She says with the pains of her wounds on her face.

The ladies began to chit chat making small talk to pass time until Anisa asks, "So what's up between you and Makeebah?"

"Thats my right hand." Aisha responds.

"How long have yall known each other?"

Not liking the direction this line of questioning was going, Aisha responds with, "Forever!" In a tone that signified she was getting irritable at the questioning.

"Relax Aisha! I'm not trying to upset you, but you might want to consider putting on gloves before washing your hands."

Not understanding what was meant by the statement Aisha asks, "What the fuck you talking about?... Why you babbling?"

With a look of disgust, mixed with fear, as well as admiration,

Anisa begins to say, "After I got the call telling me what happened,

Makeebah made a call to somebody...

I thought it was gone be trouble. And I ain't want it at my doorstep, so I signaled to her to dead that call.

She ignored me and goes into the bathroom and continue with her call.

I listened with my ear pressed to the door, all I hear is her arguing with somebody saying, is she dead, did you get the money?

I found it strange to be having that particular call at that time."

Thinking in her head it was too much of a coincidence.

"Did you ask her about it?" Aisha asks.

"No, it wasn't my place to be in her business." Anisa responds with a touch of concern in her voice.

"What else did you hear?" Aisha asks with a hint of betrayal lodge in her tone.

Not wanting to believe this could be... Aisha is crushed.

"I ain't hear all of her conversation... The pieces that stuck out I relayed to you." Anisa assured Aisha.

The ladies engage in heavy discussion about this whole situation, all the way up until the visiting hours had been concluded.

Aisha laying in her bed thinking to herself, she still couldn't believe Makeebah of all people would cross her.

She began to reflect on all the events that has happened to her since they been a team.

In all the scenarios, Makeebah could have easily fit into the solution as a probability, just as well as everybody else that surrounded her.

So for every pro, there was a con.

Aisha was in a state of limbo as to what should be her next move.

3.2 IN THE MIX

In the meantime, Makeebah was in control of the business affairs that had been handed down to her, due to Aisha's mishap.

As normal, things were running smoothly until she incorporated a new order of things.

Instead of allowing the business to grow and maximize profits, she's determined to run it into the ground.

Therefore, forfeiting the power she holds over to its rightful owner, Mujahid.

Although Aisha had invested all her time into the building of her empire, Makeebah only wanted to see nothing more than Aisha's work crumble.

With her assistance the vision was becoming more of a reality as opposed to a wishful thought.

She immediately raises the prices on material.

The partnerships Aisha created had spiraled southward.

The quality of the material had down played to the poorest of low quality.

The once orderly blocks that moved sixty percent of the material, had dwindled down to spoils of deceitful vengeance.

The hustlers that once occupied these blocks has now resorted to doing stick-ups and take downs to support the lavish lifestyle they had become accustomed to.

The throbbing pulse of the business had been reduced to a barely functioning venture.

With all the new chaos implemented, the Family had become distant cousins.

The relationships between loyal investors into the business of Aisha had become estranged.

Makeebah took all of two weeks to destroy what took months to build.

News of the crumbling had managed to surface through the wire of the circuit.

Mujahid had gotten wind of the tragedy and was thrown through a loop as to why his empire had been vanishing.

Pee-Wee approaches and explain to him that it's been a breach of contract on the part of Aisha.

The terms that Dawud had etched in stone had been violated.

He informs Mujahid that the prices are sky high and the quality of material is dirt.

"The wolves is ready to back off and sink fangs into new prey." He alerts Mujahid, referring to his lil brother Dawud and his team.

Mujahid then says to Pee-Wee, "Tell your team don't abandon ship... Give me a second to get things back in order."

Pee-Wee then replies, "This is in vain... Without the material, there is no Ten percent of profits for me.

I've got to eat in order to give this time back. These legal fees is expensive." He informs Mujahid in a tone that had been respectful, yet firmly stated.

"This me Pee-Wee... The well never runs dry. Just give me a minute to fix shit out there." Mujahid states in a tone that assured Pee-Wee that the wait would definitely be worth it.

Pee-Wee agrees to wait and embraces Mujahid as to say, I have major love for you.

Mujahid immediately puts news in the wind.

Within a matter of days, Makeebah had been up to see him.

Upon entrance into the visiting room, Makeebah had seen the expression on Mujahid face.

It wasn't pleasant at all!

He sits beside her and in an angry tone ask, "What the fuck is goin on out there?"

"What you mean?" She asks in a scared tone.

"My empire is crumbling... I thought you was holding shit down?"

"I am... I just had to tear shit down so you could rebuild the troops back up to standards." She says in a tone that said she was confident in her actions.

"Not at all... Leave things as they were.

I don't recall asking you to change shit!

I specifically told you to keep things as they were, so what's the problem?" He says sarcastically.

Then goes on to say, "I want shit back how it was. Whatever you did... Undo!

You just the eyes...

Let me take care of the thinking." He says in a voice that made Makeebah quiver from the sound of the sexiness.

She had been lost in the look in his eyes.

The only thing she could do was rectify her errors. And hold shit down for her man, so she believed in her mind.

For the remainder of the visit Mujahid had instructed her how to put the pieces back together while at the same time increasing profits.

Within a week shit was on the track of getting back to how they were.

Business was booming and profitable.

Feeling better, but still not fully recovered, Aisha is fast at heart to cipher through the turmoil that had plagued her heart.

For the past couple of weeks she's been creeped out at the notion that Makeebah had this done to her.

She never in a million years would have suspected Makeebah of all people to snake her.

Something about the whole situation just didn't sit tight in the mind of Aisha.

After long exhausting hours of thinking, Aisha decides to get to the bottom of this, to see for herself, if truth had been a fact in the thoughts she had been harboring.

She calls Makeebah and lays foundation to build the structure upon.

If in fact Makeebah had anything to do with this, then she naturally would swallow the cheese, as all rats do.

Aisha had spread the word that she had knew who shot her.

In no time at all word circulated through the streets.

Makeebah got wind of the news and decided to pay Aisha a visit.

"What's up Aisha?" Makeebah asks.

Not feeling the fact that since her first time to see her, Makeebah had yet to grace her presence again.

Aisha answers with, "I got word who did this to me." She says with certainty in her voice.

"Who is it?... How you find out?" Makeebah inquires with a touch of nervousness in her voice.

"I had a visitor who was a witness to the incident.

Had it not been for her, then I would still be in the dark." She says baiting the trap.

"A witness... Who was it? And why she just coming through now?" Makeebah responds.

"It's legit! She didn't know their names, but she seen them several times with her old man.

I got Dawud on top of that as we speak." Aisha assures her.

Trying to persuade Aisha to do the research on the information before reacting.

Makeebah decided to meet with the witness to check out the story.

Aisha refuses the assistance.

Instead told Makeebah, "Don't worry about it ... You just take care of the business. This gone be taking care of."

Then she asks Makeebah, Hand me my phone out that top drawer?"

Knowing Makeebah would see the name, number and address to the person on the paper she had planted in the drawer.

After handing Aisha the phone, Makeebah decided to leave abruptly using a bullshit excuse that she had to meet somebody for work.

A few hours later, Makeebah pulls up to the address that had been on the paper in Aisha's drawer.

She observes the residence for a while before attempting to be known.

She sees a girl come out and follows her to see where she was going.

This woman walked to the corner store to get a pack of cigarettes, Makeebah observed, as she followed the woman into the store.

Out of nowhere she cut right into the woman, "Excuse me sis... Those boots are fly. Where you cop them at?"

"I got them from Daffy's." The woman responds.

Not really caring about the boots, she just needed an entry to cut into this woman.

Makeebah began to get joe with this woman.

Then out of nowhere she brung up the shooting that happened that involved Aisha.

The woman quickly feeds into it and spews out, "That was fucked up... Dude ain't have to shoot her."

This confirmed to Makeebah that the woman had been there, or knew something about the shooting.

After briefly conversing with the woman, Makeebah leaves.

She makes her way back to her car and makes a phone call.

"We got problems!" She says to whoever she was talking to.

Then proceeds to say, "Meet me at Bobalou's in 15 minutes."

Bobalou's was a ducky bar out the way. A sure spot not to be seen by anybody of importance.

Upon getting there, she's greeted anxiously by her associate.

"What's up?" He asks with a puzzled tone.

"Somebody seen you do the work on Aisha." Makeebah informs him.

After a brief pause, allowing the data she had just gave to her associate to sink in, she then adds, "I got the bitch handle, so you can clean up your mess."

"No doubt... You sure she seen it?" He asks in disbelief.

He was conscious of his surroundings.

And positive the work was clean.

Nevertheless, he accepts the information to be on the safe side.

"It has to be done immediately, she already in cahoots with one of Aisha's shooters... It's only a matter of time before she I.D.'s you." Makeebah says with conviction and emphasis to stress the importance of the hit.

What she didn't realize was that all she's doing had been anticipated.

Aisha had planted the bait and she bit.

All the data she had was all false.

Aisha knew that if it was a witness and any truth to what Anisa had told her then Makeebah would panic.

Just as she did.

The whole time Makeebah had been followed since she left the hospital by one of Dawud's goons.

Her panic caused her to react too soon.

Bringing her accomplice out the woodworks to be seen by the many.

Now the fate of Makeebah and her associate lays within the grasp of Aisha.

Aisha receives a phone call.

Not wanting to hear the news that was about to be revealed, she braces herself for whatever may come.

"It's a go!" Dawud confirms.

"Then do what has to be done." Aisha said saddened by her own words.

A tear dropped from her eyes. And a deep breath was taken.

Then she reminded Dawud that Makeebah had to go by the hands of herself.

Even though Makeebah had snaked her, the thought of her dying at the hands of a stranger was unthinkable to her.

Aisha wanted her to know who did this to her.

Also, being closure to the question that lingered in her head, why?

After hanging up with Aisha, Dawud calls the goons that's been in pursuit of Makeebah.

He tells them too, "Stay with the associate."

Already on his heels, he follows the man to his house.

Assuming he's readying himself to get rid of the witness, the goon waits for him to make his move before doing the job required of him.

Just as the man exits his home with what appeared to be move out clothes, fatigues and leather gloves, the goon steps into him and shoves him back into the house.

Not able to get to his ratchet on his waistline, due to being taking off guard, the associate smiles and prepares to be amongst the departed.

Before the flames could be felt from the goon's gun, the associate asks, "What tipped you off?"

As part of his last rights, the goon answers, "Your partner in crime, her work was sloppy."

Then let two shots rip into the head of the associate.

Makeebah had been waiting patiently anticipating the call alerting her that the job was done.

She begins to get nervous when no call is received by midnight.

No longer able to withstand the urge to call her associate, Makeebah calls him to find out the status of the standings.

She wasn't able to get through the first couple of times she called.

She began calling every ten minutes on the hour.

After the first couple of hours it was sunk in that a problem had erupted.

Not being able to identify the problem, she speculates all the worst case scenarios.

In all the realms of her speculations, it always lead back to her.

She had known that if Aisha got wind of her part in the mayhem then war was definitely in play.

The ideal of facing off with Aisha wasn't a scary vision in Makeebah's world.

All the fear came into play when on a daily basis she has to walk on egg shells not knowing how, when, or where the drama would take place.

How the execution would be done is what scared her the most.

Instead of allowing her mind to play tricks on her, she decided to investigate and get the truth.

Trying to reach her associate one last time, but was unable to do so, she takes it upon herself to go over to his home.

As she was about to knock on the door, it blows open.

There she sees her associate lying dead in the vestibule.

Automatically, without weighing the option of somebody who he'd done dirt to had evened the score, she reacted on the assumption that Aisha had struck.

The only thing that ran through Makeebah's mind was to get to her associate's accomplice before he's trapped up and spills his guts.

She had known of him. And his work, but wasn't sure how he would hold up under the pressure of Aisha's goons.

She picks up her associate's phone and retrieves the number to his accomplice.

She places the call expecting to get him before anybody else could.

Not sure if her associate had given up the details of the plot, she prepares to hunt him down herself.

Just in case her associate stood on his actions there would be no ties left to link to the hit on Aisha.

Her patience wore thin.

And her emotions are running wild.

Ignoring the golden rule of the streets, never allow your emotions to dictate your actions, she tracks her target down to a small hole in the wall hood club out in Frankford.

Still unaware that her every move is being watched.

Had it not been for her conscious, the whole plot would've been executed with perfection.

Her insecurities allowed the light to shine on the darkness of her actions.

Makeebah walks up on the accomplice and pulls him to the side for privacy.

She informs him that her associate had been killed.

Thinking the music was altering his hearing, because what he heard he believed couldn't be correct, He grabs Makeebah's hand and leads her to a side door that lead into a parking lot for the staff of the club.

Away from the music and focused on what was to be said, he asks, "Now what you say?"

Makeebah responds with, "I said your mans is dead."

She had known he knew who she was referring to, due to the fact, that was the only tie to link her and him together.

Without the associate, her and the accomplice would never have a reason to intermingle.

"I went pass his crib and found him laid out." She finishes with uncertainty in her voice as to how much of a stand up dude he really was.

"Damn sis... You saying that like you questioning my integrity." He shoots back at her with a sensed sound of disbelief in his tone.

"Nah... I ain't saying, or questioning nothing!...

I'm trying to see if you ready to ride for the cause." She says in attempts to excite a reaction to strike back.

"You fuckin right... I'm always on board to rock out for my nigga... So what's up." He asks.

"Where you parked at?"

"That's me over there." He responds pointing to a black Lexus coupe.

"Let's rock out then." She says while waiting for him to lead the way to his car.

As he approaches his car and readies to unlock the doors, she splatters his brain matter all over the glass of his car.

Then slides out the parking lot unnoticed by anybody.

Even giving the slip to the cats that had been tailing her.

Expecting her to exit as she entered, they parked in the front across from the door.

She left through the side.

And made her way to her car that had been further behind them, closer to the corner of the block.

Feeling a lot better that there were no ties to link her to the Aisha drama.

She now only had to see where Aisha mind frame was in order to see where she had to go with this whole situation.

The very next day, Makeebah makes her way up to see Aisha.

Visiting hours hadn't even started and she was there.

Not really knowing how she wanted to address the matter, Makeebah acted as normal.

Hoping Aisha would address the situation, if in fact it was a situation.

Sensing the jittery behavior and nervousness of Makeebah, Aisha asks, "What's up! Something on your mind?"

"Nah... Why you say that?" Makeebah responds in a defensive mode.

Aisha had known the kind of snake Makeebah was.

The reality was in her face.

She could no longer deny the accusations.

Still not letting on that she had knew Makeebah had her set up, Aisha continues to keep shit as normal.

Feeling disgust and betrayal had managed to plague her feelings toward Makeebah, Aisha asks, "So how's business coming along? Ain't no problems is it?"

"Shit the same... Muthafuckas can't even tell you gone." She responds.

Makeebah begins to unwind.

The vibe she was expecting to be set was far from the actual surface.

She felt she would only be drawing on herself to keep her guard up, so she breaks down into normal Makeebah mode.

After a few hours, she spins off.

And again becomes the same Ole rotten Makeebah.

None the wiser that she was marked for death.

Although Aisha didn't bring the secret to light, the taste left behind only made things that much worser for Makeebah and her day.

Aisha had made up her mind, the once pondered question as to the method of death was made simple.

She wanted it slow, painful and tortuous.

3.3 RELATIONS OR RELATIONSHIP

Back in the swing of things, Makeebah continues to do her.

Never once giving thought to the notion that Aisha was playing her like a fiddle.

In her mind, she had been the one calling the shots.

She was the puppet master.

In the street life, its two things that should never be disregarded, never let your right hand know what the left hand is doing.

And keep your enemies close at all times.

Makeebah had neglected the rules.

And her unwillingness to follow them would eventually be her down fall.

She had been so focused on getting at Aisha that she never took notice to the fact that Anisa was on the verge of moving her out.

Throughout this whole ordeal Anisa had been the only comfort for Aisha. She was her rock.

When Aisha got depressed, it was Anisa who lifted her spirits.

When she was lonely, Anisa embraced the moment and used the opportunity to weigh heavy on her heart.

As well as the basics of a relationship.

She had been a shoulder to lean on.

A hand to hold. And an ear to listen.

Had Makeebah been around long enough to observe the whole picture, she would have seen the bond that had grown.

The physical relations had eventually graduated to an emotional state.

On her way up to see Aisha, Makeebah slides up on Anisa. "Where you on your way to?" She asks.

"To see Aisha." Anisa responds with a tone in her voice that said she had been excited.

Never giving thought to the relationship that had been cemented between Anisa and Aisha, Makeebah tells her, "Give me a holla when you get back."

"Why... What's up?" Anisa responds with a puzzled expression that made it clear she was lost by the statement.

"Chill ma... I'm just trying to see you a little later and spend some time." She says in a tone that lead Anisa to believe she wants to fuck.

"Yeah aiight." Anisa says, never even entertaining the idea. Makeebah then adds, "Don't forget."

Then sped off into the winds of the day.

Anisa still standing there in awe that she had the audacity to not even offer a ride to see Aisha.

Once she makes it to the hospital, she immediately says, "Your friend is out of pocket."

Not knowing who she was referring to, Aisha asked, "Who you talking about?" In a semi playful tone.

"Makeebah!" She responds in a tone that illustrated she had major disgust for her.

"Please... I don't even want to hear about her today." Aisha states in a tone that harmonized the same sentiments as Anisa.

Anisa then goes on to explain what happened and what was said.

Paying her no mind, Aisha changes the focus of discussion. "So you do what we talked about?"

"Mujahid?" Anisa responds.

"Who else?" Aisha says in a sarcastic tone that said of course idiot.

"I started it... I just ain't finish. You sure it's gone work?" Anisa asks with an unsure rhythm that expressed the doubts she had about the whole situation.

"We gone make it work." She says in a joking manner but at the same time Anisa had known she was serious.

"While you finishing up the first part, I need you to get on top of the second part as well." Aisha adds with a tone of seriousness in her voice.

Anisa just closed her eyes briefly and nodded her head to signify that she was on board with what Aisha wanted her to do.

The next morning, Anisa gets up and makes her way up to the prison to see Mujahid.

Only recognizing him from pictures Aisha had showed her, she waves in a way to get Mujahid's attention.

As he makes his way over to her, he's caught off guard and puzzled as to who Anisa had been.

Before he's seated he ask, "You here for me?"

With a smile that accented the features of her plain, yet, beautiful face, Anisa responds in an oh so sweet voice that gave the impression of innocence.

"Yes sir."

"Who are you... And what is it gone take to make you an asset as well as a compliment to my life?" He asks in a tone that couldn't be any clearer that he was flirting and very much interested in getting to know her.

She blushes and then proceeds to explain what the visit had been all about, "I'm Anisa... I did some business for you..."

"For me!" Mujahid says in a confused yet hostile voice.

Never factoring in that this was the chick Kay had told him about until she replies, "DNA... Hair sample... Ten grand."

With an intrigued look in his eyes, along with a snap of his fingers, he says, "My bad sis... I know who you are and what this is about."

After chuckling for a brief moment he continues, "So what's the verdict?... What I want, can it be done."

"Yes... and it's already done." She responds.

"So what now?" Mujahid asks in attempts to get a clue as to how it's gone work.

"You give me my money and I give you the sample... We part ways and forget it ever happened." She says in an almost sarcastic tone that emphasized getting her money.

"Damn... You right... I got you! I be touching in the next couple weeks... You got some type of information that I can get at you with?"

"Yeah... But I don't give my number out! Tell me when you getting out and a number, and I'll get at you then." She says with a sexy look on her face and the radiance of her beautiful smile.

"Sis... I been booked these last couple years, I been out of commission, so I ain't got a number yet... But leave me some type of information to get at you... I'm good people... Real talk!" He says in a tone that assures her he about business.

Agreeing to leave contact information, Anisa gets an ink pen from the officer's desk and writes a number in Mujahid's palm.

Ready to leave, Mujahid asks her to stay for a while.

Not really wanting to, she agrees to stay.

The conversation was interesting, but dismissed as moot.

All that ran through her mind was getting back to see Aisha.

She wanted to inform her that the bait was taken and the fish is on the hook.

Finally the visit draws to a close.

And she was free to get back to the pitter of the pat that made her heart jump and skip a beat.

Back at the hospital, Anisa is all too excited to express the relief she felt because Mujahid had accepted the bait.

She also was flattered that a man of his stature had an interest in a woman of her caliber.

Although the attention Mujahid expressed was warranted deep down inside, she chose to abandon that part of her fact findings to Aisha.

Instead kept it strictly business.

However, outside the realms of Aisha, she did drift into a place where her thoughts became her sanctuary.

His words became her comfort to help lift her self-esteem to levels undreamed of.

All her life she has suffered from low self-esteem.

Never really putting effort into a relationship. Even though the titles of boyfriend and girlfriend was always appropriately distributed.

To her it was a formality, something to keep the people from talking.

She had tried to stay out the limelight for the majority of her life. Using only her intelligence to carry her through life.

Her relationships were just as they sounded to be, strictly relations. Never injecting emotions to identify that love had lived within her soul.

For some reason Mujahid had fit the profile of what, if ever she was to get involved, her dude should be. So relishing the moment is of no value.

To her Aisha was where her allegiance was pledged.

Once she relayed her findings to Aisha, Anisa had been far from her normal self.

She was so distant that Aisha noticed the difference.

"You alright?" Aisha offers hoping to get a response that could help shed light on the hollowness of Anisa's personality.

"I'm good Boo!" She responds not wanting the emptiness she felt to be seen.

If she had to be a window at any time, this was the moment she wanted to be opaque as opposed to transparent.

Anisa would feel really awkward trying to express her interest in Mujahid to Aisha.

Especially since she had become so fond of Aisha on an emotional level.

"Are you ready for the next part?" Aisha asks in a tone that expressed she had to be committed in order to execute it to perfection.

"Of course Boo." Anisa responds in a tone that Illustrated doubt that was masqueraded as complete commitment.

Aisha grabs Anisa's hand and in her sincerest voice, she says, "This is the last step in order for us to be secure that we have equal playing field to try to grow as a unit."

The idea of having someone to love, excited as well as humbled, the raging feelings that ran wild through the most vital organ of Anisa, her heart.

Speechless at the statement that had just been made, Anisa raises Aisha's hand still interlocked with hers and rubs it against her cheek, before placing a gentle peck upon its sensuous skin.

This confirming her willingness to participate. Also, her eagerness to allow their relations to grow into a relationship.

For the next few days Anisa had been battling with herself to kill the thoughts that raced through her mind.

Unable to do so, she decided to walk on the wild side.

She phones the prison and has the administration to relay the message to have Mujahid call her.

A couple hours later she receives a call from an 814 area code hoping it was Mujahid she answers.

To her surprise it was him.

"What's up?" Mujahid asks in a voice that quickly made the thought of phone sex run through her mind.

"Nothing... I was bored and just wanted to hear your voice again." She says in a silly little girlish tone.

After pausing to allow her soul to smirk, she continues with "I been thinking about what you said... And I'm ready to be a queen... So how do I begin to prepare to be throned?" She asks in a jokingly tone.

"The first thing you have to do is... Be honest with me at all times, regardless of the situation... keep it funky and raw.

Next, you have to be the keeper of my heart...

You must protect and spare it the pains of disloyalty.

Once you get those down... We can work on everything else that may erupt." He says in a tone that symbolized sincerity.

Giddy and engulfed by the conversation of Mujahid, Anisa gets comfortable and allows her mind to be captivated.

After a few hours of conversation, it came to an end.

Mujahid had to go.

If not, she would have become a permanent fixture on her sofa.

However, he does promise to call her at least once a day to keep her content with being a potential prospect in his life.

Totally forgetting about Aisha, Anisa missed her date to spend time with her.

The phone call she had received put her in a zone that one could only dream of being in.

She found herself getting the best of both worlds.

The leadership, strength and security of being with a man.

Also, the emotional and sensual aspects of a woman, lined with the physical talents that relieved the well, when needed.

She had been in heavenly bliss for the time being.

After hearing the fact finding of Anisa's visit to Mujahid, Aisha decided to leave the hospital.

She'd rather die in the midst of battle, as opposed to just lying there like a sitting duck.

Still not capable of fulfilling her duties 100 percent, she takes her chances.

And what she can't do, she'll pay to get done.

With only a couple weeks left to Mujahid's release date, she had to get her shit in order.

Plus, she had a score to even with Makeebah.

In her mind this was a drop in the bucket compared to the real task that laid ahead of her.

She calls Anisa.

"What's up baby girl?" Aisha says with all the affection her voice could carry.

Hearing the noises of horns honking and music blaring, Anisa asks, "Where you at?"

"On my way to you." She responds.

"You wasn't supposed to be home for another month at least! What happened?" Anisa asks in a worried voice.

"I'm good... I just had to finish up unfinished business and get things prepared for the war." Aisha says with a tone in her voice that one could mistake as humor.

"You know you wrong... What good is you, if you not able to function adequately... You need to go back to the hospital and get healthy." Anisa says in a motherly tone.

"Fuck all that... Either you gone rock out with me, or you gone cut the strings!

I'm giving you the scissors... Decide what you gone do." Aisha says giving her an ultimatum to either accept the situation, or ignore it and be on her own.

Then goes on to say, "I'll be at your spot in like fifteen minutes... So have your mind made up by then."

Pulling up to Anisa's building, Aisha had to catch her breath.

She had to prepare herself for the decision that was soon to be rendered.

Once she gotten herself together, she knocked on the door expecting Anisa to answer.

But instead, she hears an argument occurring.

She lets herself in after listen for a while.

The look on Anisa's face was sheer terror to see Aisha.

Quickly she tries to masquerade the feeling as shock.

Not knowing if Aisha had heard the contents of her phone call, she immediately hangs up.

Then engage in a dramatic scene to divert the focus of her conversation to the emotional state she had been in.

Just as she expected, the ruse worked like a charm.

Aisha had disregarded any and all focus that may have been related to her call, and goes straight into the nurturing companion role.

In a sympathetic tone Aisha asks, "Who was that?"

Trying to contain her tears and wailing that Anisa had been doing, she then also adds, "What the fuck is going on?"

Anisa still not answering the question.

She just continued to play on the grieving victim role.

Once Aisha embraces her And begins to console her, she begins to speak.

"That was Kay's friend." She says still crying.

"Well... What did he want?" Aisha asks to get a clear understanding of what was going on.

"He said I owe him."

"Owe him what!... For what?" Aisha then asks in a hostile yet curious tone.

"Whatever him and Kay done before he died, he never got his cut... So now the debt fell on me, since I got possession of Kay's things." She answers in a confused and puzzled state.

Aisha began to think to herself, something doesn't sound right.

Then utters in a calm tone, "Back it up, I'm missing something...

What is it he wants?...

And what is it you owe?"

Pulling herself together Anisa replies, "He think I got some money that was left behind...

So now he wants me to give it to him...

But I don't know what he talking about, wasn't no money in all the shit he had here!"

"Who is this dude?" Aisha ask in a tone that lead Anisa to believe she would take care of it.

Anisa surrenders all the information Aisha needs to handle the problem.

"Don't worry... I got you...

He won't bother you ever again... I promise!" Aisha assures her.

This whole situation couldn't have come at a better time.

The dude was gone be the cheese in the trap for the next phase of her plan in her quest to be victorious.

Meanwhile, Makeebah was aware of the early departure of Aisha from the hospital.

Rather than avoid her, she tracks her down by phone and arrange a get together.

They had agreed to meet at a public place in Center City.

Aisha had no clue that Makeebah was protecting her own ass just in case Aisha had a grudge to settle.

Makeebah secured her protection by the law.

She knew that Aisha wouldn't act out in Center City.

Nor would her goons chance a hit in the district of the law.

The restaurant she chose was strategically centered between the Federal courthouse on 6th and Arch and the Police Headquarters, commonly referred to as the round house, at 8th and Race street.

This location would ensure her walking away unscathed from the meeting.

Word had surfaced that Aisha put money on her head.

Makeebah knew that even though it wasn't an on sight hit, it had still been a hit ordered.

Aisha didn't come out her pocket unless she really wanted you dead.

Confusion had struck Makeebah hard.

She couldn't understand, or figure out why this order was in effect?

Why she was to be brought to Aisha as opposed to just being put in the ground?

Whatever the reason was had to prevail at this meeting.

Aisha arrives on schedule.

Wasting no time with small talk, Makeebah inquired, "What's up?... We not gone play games.

you coming out your pocket to meet with me...

when all you had to do was call.

so this must be the beginning of the end...

Talk to me!...

Let me know what's the situation! "she says in a nonchalant tone with a smirk on her face.

"I..."

Before she could get the words out, Makeebah cuts her off and immediately states, "Stop the bullshit... It's me Aisha!"

Staring her in the eyes and seeing all the betrayal and deceit that lies within her heart, Aisha says, "Bitch you want it raw... I'm a give it to you raw!...

You snaked me...

That shit was foul!!!

After all the shit I done for you...

You do me like that!

I just want to know why?"

Noticing the undeniable hurt in Aisha's words, Makeebah tries to plead, "I didn't, you my dog... I would never cross you...

Whoever has planted this seed in your head is trying to divide and conquer... Don't let them win."

Ashia had known from that moment that any further conversations would be pointless.

All that ran through her mind was, this bitch is rotten to the core.

She tells Makeebah in a sincere, yet, betrayed toned voice, "We go back too far... So far me to allow you to die in the street like a dog is not gone happen...

But... I'm a kill you... I can't let it ride."

With a stare that let Makeebah know she meant her words, she gets up and leaves the restaurant. Never once looking back.

The face that she left seeing, was the face she wanted her to remember while she was slowly taking the breath out her body.

Makeebah had gotten her answer.

It wasn't no turning back now.

The once alright relationship they shared had been severed.

However, not really concerned about that because she had known Aisha's days was numbered as well.

The only thing that had her stuck was, she didn't want to betray Mujahid's wishes by killing Aisha.

This was the only joy she had to offer him.

She refused to take that away.

Therefore, out of respect for her love interest, she decided to go underground and lay low until the time was right to surface.

Whenever the time was right, she couldn't help but to think, it was gone end with a fairy tale ending.

Her getting her Knight in shining armor.

And being whisked off into the horizons of the sunset happily ever after.

In reality this act of nobleness wasn't landing her no closer to getting Mujahid than she already had been.

She just didn't realize he didn't look at her in the same light as he would another chick with potential to be wifey.

3.4 CAUGHT UP

Anxiously anticipating his return back to society, Mujahid found it extremely difficult to sleep his last eight hours away.

All that ran through his mind was the satisfaction of slaying the bitch that betrayed him.

The one whom he trusted, took a vow to cherish, now death was surely about to do them part.

The fact that Aisha had him arrested was already a hard pill to swallow.

Yet, because of his love for her, he digested and swallowed all the extras that compromised his manhood and beliefs he lived by.

She drew blood on the family he not only built, but shared bloodlines with as well. There was no way her actions could be overlooked.

He laid in his bed infatuated by all the tortuous ways to rid the earth of a piece of shit like her.

He came to the realization that what he had planned would be the better method, as well as the safest.

Although the consequences for the services he was to provide were costly, he felt they were worth it.

However, the thought of spending the rest of his natural days in a human kennel just ain't balance out in his mind.

The lingering aroma of death and blood that filled the air in which he was breathing, had managed to leave a taste in his mouth, as well as, a thirst in his heart for the soul of Aisha.

At the same exact moment within the boundaries of Philadelphia, laid Anisa, suffering from the same syndrome of sleep deprivation.

She had been torn as to who her allegiance would be pledged to.

She had been emotionally attached to Aisha, but mentally drawn to Mujahid.

Something about the aura of his presence had her stuck in a realm that she found it hard to escape.

She had straddled both sides of the fence.

A journey she had dreaded accepting.

She knew she was the key to both sides of the war.

All she had to do was decide who would be more beneficial to her growth and development as a woman.

Even after weighing the pros and cons of the situation, she had still been deadlocked.

She resorted to finding answers in a bottle of Grey Goose.

Not realizing that the bottom of the bottle only bring more problems than answers.

She ponders the endeavors she had planned in life.

A costly voyage.

Both individuals had enough money to carry her through Therefore, she found that line of thinking to be asinine.

She then begins to envision the extremities of having her life's work caught up in an emotional battle within herself, due to the lifestyle of Mujahid.

No matter how beautiful the thought may be to have a man of his stature to call her own, she'll always be the mistress to his first love, The streets.

Something Aisha couldn't foretell.

The thought of being emotionally tied to a bitch that at any time wouldn't think twice about having her so called loved one's erased from existence was scary.

She couldn't control who her heart chose.

She had the mindset to know she couldn't allow her heart to do the thinking for her.

Then there was the fantasy she couldn't erase from her mind.

She really wanted her little pussy pounded and stretched to capacity by this massive amount of man.

The thought alone had her ready to cum.

Plenty of alcohol, yet, still no answers.

Whatever she was gone do had to be done immediately.

She was only hours away from deciding her fate.

Meanwhile on the other side of town, Aisha had been on a mission to bring closure to the situation of her sister's death.

With all the information to the cat who had been in cahoots with Kay to slay her heart, she mounts up her goons and mans the battlefield.

Before rolling out she made it perfectly clear to her squad that, "there was to be no spared souls. As many casualties as needed to get this pussy. I already paid a mill for his and whoever around him soul."

Just as they pull up to the intended address of their focus, Dawud notices a cat that fit the description entering the residence.

Without hesitation he walks up to this man and commences to pistol whipping this person, until this man is laying damn near lifeless and drenched in a pool of blood.

Once unconscious, he drug the man to his vehicle and threw him in the trunk, per orders of Aisha.

Dawud couldn't understand why?

He wanted to handle the problem on sight, but Aisha had other plans.

He calls Aisha and reports his findings.

He was then instructed to take him to a house up North.

Not questioning the request, he does as he's told.

Last night had been a busy night for Aisha.

As she awakens to face the dramatic adventures of the day, she's once again feeling nervous.

She knew that if today didn't go as she planned, Mujahid wouldn't spare no cost to see her bellied up in the Schuylkill river.

She calls Anisa.

Not getting no answer, she begins to get frustrated.

Then out of the blue Anisa answers.

"Hello." She says still hung over from the melee of last night.

"Get up... It's time to get into action.

I need what should of been here yesterday." Aisha says in a serious tone.

"My bad... I meant to drop it off, but I got caught up." Anisa responds feeling like she had to earl.

"I'll be pass there in a hot minute... So be up." Aisha demands of Anisa.

After hanging up with Anisa, Aisha calls Dawud.

In a half sleep groggy type voice he answers.

"Yo... What's up?"

"Wake up." She responds.

Then proceeds to ask, "Is everything in place for me today?"

"I did everything you told me to do to the letter." He assures her before hanging up to drift back off into La La land.

With all her key elements in place, Aisha begins her journey to get at Mujahid.

By this time he should be ready to walk out the door of the prison, she thought to herself.

With that in mind she readies herself to give him a coming home present he'll never forget.

A couple hours later, Mujahid had been elated to be back in the grasp of the city he deemed to be his.

Ready to partake in all the things he had done without for the last two years, He stops at an Italian Bistro to get a full course meal.

Italian had been his favorite food.

Being from South Philly, surrounded by the infamous mafia, it was like he was forced to indulge in their cuisine.

Once done he decides to take in the new sights while indulging in the luxury of shopping.

He had a lot on his plate, not to mention a date with destiny.

After taking in the last of his little minute to get the feeling of confinement out his system, he calls the first of many who was sure to get a piece of the rock.

It just so happened to be Anisa.

She answers in an irritated tone, "What is it?"

"Calm down miss lady... A queen remains humble at all times."

He tells her.

Just hearing the sound of the voice, she had known who it was.

The irritation seemed to vanish from her voice.

A tone of excitement had managed to reinvent her as she asks, "So what do I owe the pleasure of this early morning quickie?" Referring to a quick couple minute phone call.

She had known he had rituals he had done in the morning, so if he calls, it wasn't for long.

"I'm home."

Before he could add anything to the statement, he heard a brief gasp of breath come from Anisa, followed by, "You serious."

Still feeling down from her last night's escapades, Anisa had forgotten today was the day he came home.

"You ready for me... Or do you need some time to prepare?" Mujahid asked.

Hearing nothing but chuckles while visualizing the beautifulness of her smile, he awaits a response to give him the green light to break her off a little something.

"Nah... I'm ready!"

Accepting this as an invitation to come through, Mujahid assures her he had been on his way.

Anisa immediately gets herself together.

Still confused as to who she wanted to be with, but was gone take full advantage of the moment.

She really anticipated the first shot to be nice.

In her mind, she had it all mapped out to turn Mujahid out.

Never giving thought to the idea he may really have the magic stick. And in fact, she could be the one turned out.

The time was nearing for both theories to be tested.

She was well up to the challenge.

Upon arriving at Anisa's apartment, Mujahid had stopped off and copped a viagra.

He had been through this scenario many times.

He refused to be one of those one and done type dudes.

All the rap she given him while he was inside, he was damn sure gone see if all she said, she does.

Pulling up to Anisa's building, Mujahid pays the taxi driver and hops out anticipating the treasures that was promised.

Once Anisa opens the door, he's shocked at how much different she had been in person.

On visits she was a laid back conservative meek young lady. Never once implanting the impression that behind closed doors, she could be the whore type freak that most men desired to have.

She had been standing there in nothing but a thong that her soft coco brown ass seemed to devour.

And a bra that really accented the voluptuousness of her perky pretty brown breast.

Her body had been glistening like she was already hot just awaiting the moment someone would douse her flames.

Speechless at how radiant she had been on her own playing field, he couldn't help but to be relieved he had popped a viagra.

The things that ran through his mind from the way she looked assured him that the next few hours were gone be worth the wait.

Once he accepted the invitation to enter, things became crazy.

Soon as the door closed, he found himself back against it, pants pulled to his ankles.

Not expecting the aggressiveness Anisa was demonstrating, Mujahid stood in awe fearful to move.

He felt like prey being attacked by a cougar.

Anisa had been in awe as well.

She never anticipated the surprise she had just received.

Once she dropped to her knees, she couldn't believe the size of the work she had to deal with.

All the aggressiveness had come to a halt.

Allowing herself to regain her courage to attack the massiveness of Mujahid, all she could think to herself was, Damn!

It's limp. I hope I can handle it erect.

Ignoring the approach with caution sign that echoed in her head, she proceeded to take Mujahid into her mouth.

Having trouble due to the girth, she begins to question if he's really that big, or was her mouth just that small.

Determined to perform the task she had set out to do, she reinvent her techniques to cater to the man she had been dealing with.

The mere sight of Mujahid fully erect made her hesitant to embark on the journey that laid ahead.

She knew she had to be comfortable in order to perform effectively.

She leads Mujahid into the bedroom.

The whole time she had been remembering all the many times she watch her porn.

She always told herself, if ever she was able to have what the starlets of adult movies was getting, she would own the moment and she be a 'G' about it.

Now faced with the talents of a porn star, she's petrified to think of the damage that could be done to her little pussy.

Knowing she was in control, Anisa dictates the pace, leaving Mujahid rendered submissive.

Back in play finishing the job she had started in the living room.

Once she got her rhythm, Mujahid couldn't help but to be taken aback.

Feeling the sensations brewing from deep within his loins, he braces himself for the eruption that was about to erupt.

Offering a warning to Anisa.

"Oh shit... It's... It's... Cummin! Aaaah!"

Still holding him in her mouth, she jerks him until every

last drop had been spent. Swallowing all the juices from his loins.

Now is when the real adventures begin is the look she illustrated with her eyes.

It's been too long since she had dick.

And even longer since she had hoped good dick.

She had hoped Mujahid was able to twerk the love muscle.

And just wasn't big for nothing.

Fuck all the debating and speculation, she thought to herself, it was time to sail the ocean.

She eases herself down to the stern of the ship, never believing that she would be able to take him in full.

It had been a tight, extremely tight fit.

The juices she released made the canal dilate enough to not hurt herself.

Once she realized she was able to take him to capacity, she began to get buck wild with him.

Bouncing, bending, spinning, flipping and twisting herself up like a pretzel.

She put herself in positions that almost seemed impossible to do.

She was in complete control, working Mujahid like a part time slave.

Mujahid had been shocked at how well she performed.

She definitely lived up to the hype she created.

He was fucked up that he ain't take two viagras for this young bitch. She was an animal in every sense of the word.

She was somebody he could see himself getting caught up in.

While Mujahid had been laid up with Anisa, Aisha was out taking care of business.

She had killed the dude Dawud kidnapped.

With the help of Anisa, she has staged the perfect murder.

Afterwards dousing the clothing of the victim with the tube of blood that Anisa had formulated.

Aisha had been killing three birds with one stone.

She got the revenge she sought for his part in her sister's death.

She rid Anisa of the troubles of him harassing her.

Plus, tied Mujahid into a murder that he had no knowledge of.

This way, if she was to die by the hands of Mujahid, he still had her mark of destruction for him to remember her reign by.

Aisha was by no means under estimating the abilities of Mujahid. She knew he was home. It was just a matter of time before his hunt for her pursued.

35 TIL DEATH DO US PART

Awakened by the streams of sunlight seeping through the partially drawn blinds, Mujahid looks over and sees Anisa still asleep.

Humble and peaceful, so serene, almost like a heavenly angel had fallen from the skies and landed with the grasp of his clutches.

He kisses her forehead and eases out the bed.

Although last night was a hell of a home coming for him, the moment had passed.

And it was now time to commit to the task he had envisioned for so long.

From the bathroom he found his way to the living room.

He walks around and inspects the room, almost like he was looking for something.

For what he had no clue.

However, the things he was seeing lead him to believe that Anisa was a wholesome, classy chick.

No indication that the beautiful woman he had allowed to service him in a way he's never been serviced, could have an interest in the comforts of a woman.

He makes his way to her sofa to use the phone.

He had decided to call a few of his players to spread the news he had been home.

Just as his man Dame answers his phone, Anisa awakes and picks up the phone in the bathroom to eavesdrop in on the call.

Holding the mute button so that the noise of her breathing couldn't be heard, she listens to the conversation to keep one up on Mujahid.

Surprisingly to her, the majority of the conversation had been about her.

She had been elated that Mujahid had been feeling her in the way he was.

She overheard him tell his friend.

"The shorty I'm wit is a beast... She definitely wifey material."

With nothing but smiles on her face, she thinks to herself, I really put it on that nigga.

"Chill baby boy... You just coming home... So that first shot of pussy gone be like a T-bone steak to a starving Ethiopian.

Play your hand for a minute before committing yourself to her." Dame says in a serious tone trying to prevent Mujahid from getting sprung on Anisa.

"I feel you, but sis different...

She in a league by herself... Real talk!

Shorty on some grown woman shit!

She the type of bitch a nigga need right now!" Mujahid says to Dame in a tone that leads him to believe Anisa could really be working with something.

"Whenever you decide to come up for air and get out and about, get at me... You know where I'm at... Mines ain't change." Dame says in a more pleasant tone alerting Mujahid that he wanted to link up.

"I got a few things to handle first... Then I'm at you."

Mujahid says before signing off with the hood anthem, "one."

Attempting to make another call, but got side tracked by noise of Anisa waking up.

Hurrying to meet her as she opens her eyes, Mujahid ask," Rough night sleepy head."

With a smile on her face, rather than verbalize her response, she smiles and nods her head indicating a yes.

"I went in the living room to use the horn cause I ain't want to wake you...

You looked so peaceful sleeping...

I hope that was cool?" He asks.

"stop playing.... Anything I have you have access to." She replies in a tone that suggested she was wide open to the notion that him and her could one day become strongly unified and become an us.

She sits on the edge of the bed and tells him, "My intention was to cook you a home cooked breakfast...

But you beat me up."

"Don't let that stop you...

A nigga still hungry." He says in a playful but serious tone.

As she rose to prepare to bless him with some home cooking, he couldn't help but to get excited at how lovely her ass looked. He felt himself getting excited all over again, but exercised discipline, because he knew he had business to take care of.

Fucking with Anisa he knew he wouldn't make it out the door.

For some reason he felt this young girl had the whip appeal.

A few hours later, fully nourished and ready to face the day, Mujahid gets on his way. And promised her he'll be back.

Pulling up on a group of men that he once ran with, Mujahid parks up and gets out to kick it for a brief minute.

While doing so, one of the men comes out of left field with a remark that left Mujahid baffled and angry.

"Your misses the boss of the city... Don't shit move without her say so." The man said.

Never responding Mujahid just gave him a look that said get your mind right.

Mujahid then asks, "Who got a phone on them?"

Accepting the phone from another man in the group he calls Aisha.

Not recognizing the number, Aisha answers in a tone that could be read as confusion.

"Who this?" she asked.

"Who you want it to be?" Mujahid responds in a tone that suggested he had the upper hand.

"I ain't got no time for games." She responds in an irritated tone.

"Damn... So you ain't got no time for your husband?"

"Mujahid? You been home since yesterday... So where you been? Laying up with one of your trifling ass whores?" She responds in a tone that said she really didn't care to know, nor did she wish to have this conversation at all.

Not really wanting to engage in the topic of discussion she had struck an interest in, Mujahid passes and says, "We need to talk... Meet me at the dog house for lunch."

"For what! We can talk now." She says not trusting a face to face meeting.

"Just be there... Don't make me come looking for you please!" Mujahid says before hanging up.

Aisha had rehearsed this moment over and over again in her head. Now that it was actually reality, she was nervous.

As if she was coming face to face with the grim reaper.

She didn't want to drag it out, so she prepared herself to meet him.

Prior to getting there, she was gone have her team in play, just in case he tried anything crazy.

Mujahid was too unpredictable.

He had game for days.

Everybody loved him.

And he always had soldiers that was willing to sacrifice a kamikaze mission.

She had to be real careful not to misplace her anger, causing Mujahid to react.

She calls Dawud.

Once he answers, she immediately begins to say, "We on for today...

Be at the Doghouse by 11:30... Don't play me close, but observe the blitz.

Time to rock out."

After a brief pause, she then continues and adds, "Bring all the heavy hitters... This a major move here."

"Be easy... We on it." Dawud responds assuring her he was on board for whatever.

Feeling a little more at ease knowing that her squad gone come through for her, Aisha began to countdown the minutes until noon. She had it in her mind that it wasn't gone be no discussions, it was all on sight action.

On the other hand, Mujahid had wanted the verbalization to bring closure to the question that haunted his soul, why?

He felt he was the best husband he could be due to his circumstances.

At the same time he blamed himself for the chaotic activities.

Had he stuck to the script, things wouldn't have played out as they did, or so he believed.

His first mistake was bringing his work across the threshold of his home. He knew that was a no-no.

However, in his quest to accommodate his husbandly duties and his secret affairs with the streets, he disregarded the rules, believing the consequences was far beyond his scope.

Which in turn violated the ultimate sin of the game. He introduced his wife to a life that gracefully swallowed the best of men alive.

Never giving thought to the notion, that once one absorbed the life, they become the life.

It's an addiction, no different than those that smoke coke, or snort powder.

In fact, street life is a far worse addiction.

As a hustler you prey on the sickness of others and prosper from their short comings.

If not careful, the greed will eventually turn the average into a crab, never wanting to see the next man get a head.

As one try to rise, there's always someone trying to snatch him back down to use their persons as a stepping stone so one can get themselves up.

Aisha fell victim to the glitz and glamour, never anticipating the behind the scenes work that caused the game to shine like it did.

Once faced with the adversities of such, she was lost within herself, with no clue as to how to escape.

Mujahid knew he had created this beast.

And it was his duty to slay his creation.

The only thing that made it so much more difficult was he still deep down in his heart, seen Aisha as the humble, obedient, docile individual he had first met.

Although her actions proved to be a totally different person, he was still in love.

Nevertheless, he had a job to do. And it was gone get done.

After pondering the situation and feeling a sigh of relief that he was finally gone get the closure needed to move on, he looks down at his watch and notices it was almost time to meet Aisha.

He had wrapped up his frivolous conversations with the group of men he was being entertained by and heads for the Doghouse.

Arriving at the Doghouse, he notices the avenue had been poppin.

Shocked at how shit had changed so drastically in the couple years he was down.

When he left the avenue was a hot spot, but nothing like he returned to find.

Bitches was everywhere.

Niggas was posted on the ave doing them.

There had been a beat cop patrolling on foot, up and down the avenue.

For the most part, it was like he wasn't even there. His presence ain't stop shit.

In fact, all he did was collect checks from all the different squads that used the ave as a meal ticket.

Eight and skate with a check to vacate, was his motto on a daily basis.

Long as the drama didn't occur, he ain't give a fuck about the niggas that grinded on the ave.

The things Mujahid was seeing made his mind fast forward through thoughts.

He began to allow his hustler's instincts to take control.

He already was orchestrating locking down areas of the avenue with the line he had.

In no time, he would be back at the top of the pile.

The city would again belong to him.

Bringing him back from the semi dazed state he'd been caught up in, Mujahid hears his name being called.

As he turns to see who had been calling him, all he heard was what sounded like cannons going off.

The sky went black.

He felt the arteries in his body begin to shut down. And the stoppage of his heart before he hit the ground.

Laid out in the middle of the avenue, as people crowded around to see who had been hit, somebody yells out, "That's Mujahid."

In the midst of all the chaos all that could be heard was somebody screaming for an ambulance.

The whispers throughout the crowd told the story.

As always with prying eyes, the events were taken over by speculations.

For those who seen, didn't see.

And for those who didn't see, had the most rap about what just happened.

Once the whispers in the crowd simmered down and came to a halt, speculation had the city buzzing.

At the center of all the buzzing was Aisha's name.

She had been relieved it went down, but at the same time puzzled, because it wasn't her work that executed her vision.

Prior to getting there for the meeting, Mujahid had already been laid out.

To see his body actually laying there drenched in his own blood was a horrendous sight to see, even for her.

Whoever had done this was heartless and had no respect whatsoever for the law.

Nor the capabilities of Aisha.

Even though she had wanted nothing more than to see Mujahid's blood spilled, the fact that another had done it, made her boil with rage.

Her husband had been shot down in the streets like a dirty dog.

Anisa had been home watching television when Aisha arrived.

As always when she's upset, Aisha looks to Anisa for the comfort and support she desires.

In a hysterical rage Aisha cries out loud.

The sound she let escape her soul, sounded like a wounded baboon.

Holding Aisha in her arms, Anisa just sat there allowing the hurt and resentment she felt to come out as needed.

After a while, Aisha pulls herself together and begins to tell Anisa what happened.

In a confused hazy stare, Anisa was breathless that Aisha had reacted as she did to the news of Mujahid.

In all the time she's known her not once did Aisha ever have a good thing to say about Mujahid.

In fact, she had known Aisha wanted him dead herself.

What's the problem? Was all that echoed in Anisa's mind.

To see Aisha react as she was, really made Anisa question her importance to Aisha.

It's evident that the love Aisha had for Mujahid outweighed the love she held for her.

In an uncertain tone Anisa asks, "So where do we go from here?"

With a look of disgust, that questions the audacity she had to ask a question like that at the present time.

Then finds the strength to ask, "Are you serious?" In a tone that said bitch you shot out.

Aisha then gets up and leaves Anisa's place of residence in a hostile fury.

Anisa just had her world collapse in on her.

To actually hear Aisha's response felt like she was the one who had been shot.

Her soul quivered and the love she thought was shared between her and Aisha had been vacated.

Feeling abandoned and betrayed she makes a call.

While dialing the number, all she could say to herself was, I did it again.

Referring to the way she had opened herself and personal life up to be exploited and walked upon as a doormat.

After her last experience at trying to get the love she not only desired, but deserved as well, she vowed to never allow herself to be put in a predictament like the one she had found herself in once again.

She begins to ask in a winy sniffling tone to whomever she called, "Can I have the number to temple hospital please."

News of Mujahid's attack managed to find its way to the eardrum of Makeebah.

Feeling saddened that Aisha had struck and killed the love of her life, she flew into a rage and automatically vows to put Aisha in a casket that would touch the bottom of the ocean's floor.

Holding true to her word to Mujahid, Makeebah allowed Aisha to live as long as she did.

Without him there to mediate the beef between the two, Makeebah sees it as an open invitation to get that bitch.

After all Mujahid done for her, she had the nerve to spill his blood.

Loyalty brings trust and character.

Ungratefulness breeds envy and jealousy.

Fucking with a bitch heart is a recipe for death.

Aisha signed her own death warrant in the eyes of Makeebah

3.6 DIE BITCH

Still saddened by the news of Mujahid's ambush, Makeebah rushes back to the city.

The whole ride she had contemplated all the many things she had wanted to do to Aisha.

She envisaged many ways to die.

The only problem was choosing one.

It had to be appropriate for a rotten bitch.

The method was uncertain, but one thing that was for sure, Aisha was gone die.

In order to get at Aisha like she wanted, Makeebah knew she had to pierce the layers of goons Aisha had protecting her.

The one rule she had always remembered was, sever the head and the body will fall.

With that in mind, she targeted Dawud.

She knew he was the one calling the shots to the rest of the goons.

Therefore, whatever was gone be done had to revolve around the slaying of Dawud.

It's only been a couple of weeks since Makeebah went underground.

She knew Aisha didn't change her routines that abruptly.

For the most part, her schedule would fairly be similar to the one she had been used to.

For Makeebah to pull this off she would need some assistance.

Stuck in thought as to who would be her best choice to help her get close to Aisha and her team.

Then after a few minutes in thought, it hits her like a ton of bricks.

If anybody was in a position to get the job done, it would have to be Anisa.

She had managed to build a bond that went outside the realms of the normal relationship between girlfriends.

In her heart, Makeebah believed it had in fact, taken on the identity as being personal.

She had noticed the secrecy that occurred between Anisa and Aisha.

The look of happiness that surfaced when in the company of one another.

If ever she had to epitomize the essentials of a perfect couple, next to her and Mujahid, it would have to be those two.

After strategically planning how to get Anisa to play along without bringing attention to her plan, she finally calls Anisa.

After a few attempts, Anisa answers. "Hello."

"What's up miss young booty?" Makeebah says in a tone that Anisa had no trouble identifying.

"What you want? I'm busy." Anisa responds in a really hostile tone that left the impression she didn't want to be bothered.

"Relax boop!... I got something you definitely can use, but first you got to put yourself in a position to be able to prosper from the events."

After allowing that to seep in, Makeebah then adds, "You in or not?"

Anisa paused briefly, then disturbing the silence that had been rendered she says, "I ain't for no snake shit... And I'm not fucking nobody."

Music to Makeebah's ears.

With a smile big enough to see every tooth in her mouth, she begins to explain the contents of her scheme.

Hearing the requirements needed from her to execute the plan Makeebah had, Anisa couldn't help but to think to herself, this bitch is diabolical.

Not knowing exactly why Makeebah needed her to participate, or what the ultimate end result would bring, Anisa sets off to do her part.

Makeebah felt that this was only a necessary step in order to get closer to her end goal.

Her next step would take expert timing to get the pieces in place to move forward.

Feeling extremely depressed about her husband, Aisha been laid up in an antisocial state. She wasn't her normal self. This whole scenario had taken its toll on her.

She begins to reflect back upon all the events that happened.

And all the losses she's taken due to her involvement in the game. She can't help but question, where did she go wrong.

In a deep meditative state, when suddenly she's brought back to current times with the sounds of her phone ringing.

She didn't want to answer it, but at the same time, she didn't want to let on that she was going through shit.

A chain is only as strong as its weakest link.

Without her, the whole operation was done.

Once she got around to answering the phone, it had been Anisa.

In an apologetic voice she says, "Hey boo... I just wanted to apologize for the rudeness of my behavior.

I didn't realize that you were really going through something about Mujahid.

Had you let me know you was still in love with him...

Things would have played out a lot different had I known my role. And played my lane as I was supposed to."

"No... It was my fault... I didn't realize I felt as I did until then." Aisha says in a sympathetic tone.

"So we cool again?" Anisa asks in an unsure voice.

"Yeah... We good!" Aisha responds.

"Good! I got a friend who trying to do some business with you.

I told him I would take a minute to holla at you and see what's what."

"What kind of business we talking?" Aisha asks.

"He wants to step in your line of work...

I'm just supposed to bring everybody together. yall can talk when yall get there." Anisa says in a confused tone.

"We'll see... I'll arrange for Dawud to meet with him."

"Do I call him to find out when he free, or do you just give him a time?" Anisa asks.

"I'll call you back in a couple, to let you know when and where." Aisha says indicating she'll do business with this person.

Once Aisha hangs up with Anisa, she immediately calls Dawud.

"What's up baby boy... How you making it?"

"I'm good!... Shit doing what it do... Numbers out the ballpark!" Dawud responds in a happy tone that said he was having it his way.

"Good... I need you to get with a cat and pull him into the ranks for me." Aisha says.

"Who is it? What's his range?" He asks in a voice that lead Aisha to believe he wasn't really into the quest, but on the strength of her, he'll do it.

"He a good friend of my peoples... I'm a just bring yall together and play from there." She says.

Then after a brief pause asks, "So what's good for you?" Referring to a time that would best suit him.

"Any time after 10 am." He responds.

"Well I'm a set it up for about 3pm tomorrow at the spot." She says in a tone that said it's cool, take care of my peeps.

"Got you ma!" He responds before hanging up.

Aisha had a feeling that just didn't sit right with her.

For one, Anisa had never came at her on the tip of trying to be a middle man.

Secondly, she didn't know the quality of the character of the cat who was to meet Dawud.

It just ain't feel kosher, the whole transaction.

However, her greed allowed her to go along with the deal as long as a profit was involved for her.

She then calls Anisa back and set up the meeting.

Never giving it a second thought.

Aisha fell back into her depressive state.

Anisa had come through for Makeebah.

The rest was up to Makeebah to handle.

Makeebah prepared to do what she needed to in order to fulfill her goal once Anisa gave her the heads up that the score had been fixed.

The very next day Makeebah had gotten up extra early to get in position.

She knew Dawud would be expecting a high yellow cat with rainbow gators.

As he sat patiently waiting for the ghost figure to arrive, she just had to creep him and then sleep him.

A task that seemed all too easy.

However, she never took into account that Aisha would be playing shot gun and watching Dawud's back.

Once Makeebah arrived at the location to get the drop on Dawud,

She was taken by surprise.

Already sitting there in a tinted up S.U.V was Aisha.

The sight of Makeebah sparked a rage within her that took her outside the character of her normal self.

As Makeebah walked alongside her car, on the opposite side of the street, Aisha couldn't control the fury and jumped out her car and let off a host of shots in attempt to hit Makeebah.

The sound of shots created a panic on the block they had been parked on.

Not knowing where the shots was coming from, Dawud slumps down in his seat, reaches for his pistol, while opening his car door he slides out of the vehicle he had been in to get a better look at what was going on.

Makeebah took cover behind a van that had been a foot, or so in front of her.

Everybody remained planted until the first break in the shots.

That's when everybody peeked to see where the shots was coming from.

As well as who was bussing their gun.

Once her clip was empty, Aisha squats down behind the S.U.V she was in and reloads.

Dawud noticed Aisha, but couldn't see no target for her to hit, so automatically he returns fire, believing that Aisha was taking shots to do him in.

Aisha screams in a panic once she heard the whistling of bullets whizzing pass her head, "Dawud what you doing!"

"You trying to push my wig back... It ain't goin down like that." He responds still letting the four pound he had roar.

"It's not for you, she behind you." Aisha says trying to warn him and cease fire on her own self.

As he turned to see who Aisha had been referring to, a shot hits him in the face.

Before he could react, a second shot hit him in the neck.

He grabbed his neck to stop the bleeding while gasping for air.

Makeebah creeps up along the side of him and ends his suffering with an execution style hit between the eyes.

Then grabs his gun.

She knew his four pound could do more damage than the .380 she had.

By this time, Aisha was reloaded and made her way around the truck until she was in front looking through the windshield.

Makeebah had managed to make her way to the back side of the S.U.V.

Looking through the back windshield to pick a clean shot, she falls to the ground and lets one shot whistle through the shin of Aisha from down low underneath the car.

Refusing to let Makeebah get another shot off, Aisha falls to the side, being shielded by the front left tire.

She quickly lets off a cluster of shots to buy time while she dragged herself to the front of the car that had been in front of hers.

Makeebah knew Aisha was hit and couldn't go but so far.

She laid low counting shots until she felt Aisha was unloaded.

Then she made her way up onto the car Aisha had been hiding behind and says, "Bitch... If you not at peace with your maker, you better patch shit up, cause you ready to meet him." In a tone that kind of resemble the antics of a mad scientist.

Aisha let off two more shots, then slides down the side of the car on the blind side.

Makeebah count is at ten.

Waiting for the last one to ring out before she made her move.

She had known Aisha's weapon of choice was an eleven shot .380.

Just as she was about to let off a shot to force Aisha's hand to release that last shot, Aisha pops from around the side and lets her last shot rip through the back of Makeebah.

Not able to feel her limbs, Makeebah laid paralyzed crying out, "I can't feel my legs! I can't move!"

Aisha grabs the gun that Makeebah had dropped and puts it in Makeebah's mouth.

Over the mumbles that tried to escape despite the barrel being in her mouth, Aisha pulls the trigger.

Unable to walk, Aisha crawls back to her vehicle and sped off.

She was in need of medical attention, but couldn't go to the hospital.

Her first thought was to go to Anisa and let her patch her up.

Once she gets to Anisa building, she calls to make her aware of what she needed her to do.

Anisa comes out and tends to Aisha.

once she got her into her apartment The pain pills Anisa had given her put Aisha out like a light.

Forty-eight hours later, Aisha awakens from the ordeal that landed her in the realms of Anisa's world.

She had been tied down to the bed she was in.

She felt like she had been the one who was paralyzed from the shootout.

She over hears Anisa on the phone in the next room.

She had been talking to a physician regarding Mujahid's condition.

At first Aisha thought she was in some sick twisted dream.

All this time she had believed and come to grips with the fact, or idea that Mujahid was dead, now in the time of her crisis she finds out he's alive.

That blew her mind.

She begins to scream franticly for Anisa.

As Anisa enters the room nonchalantly, she stuffs Aisha's mouth with some sort of cotton fabric to muffle the screams.

Then leaves back out the room to continue her phone call.

Aisha laid there scared out her mind, not understanding what was going on.

The innocence that once graced Anisa's face had been forfeited.

The look that replaced it, was pure evil.

Her eyes no longer resembled the twinkling of a star.

Her stare had become cold.

And darkness fell from within her pupils.

Aisha had recognized that look.

It was a transformation that she had once simulated.

She had been confused though.

Anisa wasn't in a position that allowed the game to absorb her, so for her to transform into the being she had become, was shocking.

Still trying to muster up the strength to free herself from bondage, Aisha exhausted all that was left within the core of her being.

Tired and in pain she never felt before, Aisha just laid there allowing all sorts of scenarios entertain her mind.

Every horror movie she's had ever seen had managed to play out in her head.

All ending with her being the victim of torture.

Just as she had gotten a second burst of wind to try to undo the restraints that held her, Anisa enters and just stares at her.

After a brief moment of silence, Anisa begins to speak.

"I bet you wondering what's going on... No need to worry... It'll all be revealed in due time." She said while walking towards Aisha with a syringe filled with some sort of solution.

She then injects Aisha with this solution.

Aisha immediately embraced the feelings this solution rendered to her.

She felt relaxed, free and careless as to whatever was going on.

Within seconds she drifted off into the solemn slumber in which she had awaken.

Anisa had secured the restraints even more, then prepared herself to leave.

3.7 OH WHAT A WEB SHE'S WOVEN

Driving, anticipating telling Mujahid the web of deceit she entangled herself in, Anisa begins to ponder just how to do so.

She had woven a web that would be extremely difficult to untangle.

In her mind, it never played out as it had come to be.

She was supposed to come out on top, not trapped in a war within herself between her heart and mind.

She allowed her powerful influence to manipulate others.

Take control of her.

And go beyond the scope of her expectations.

It originally began as a ploy to get a nice piece of change out of Aisha.

Once Kay had put her on the scheme, Anisa became greedy.

She manipulated the thoughts of Aisha to believe that Kay had kidnapped and killed her little sister, knowing she would want vengeance.

She used the power of persuasion to enhance the thought, as well as get rid of Kay, to be able to keep the money to herself.

Since Kay told her Mujahid's plot, Anisa stalked Aisha until she had an opportunity to ease her way into the circle of trust.

The only way she seen fit, was to betray the efforts of Mujahid.

It initially wasn't intended to be a kidnapping homicide.

She was just supposed to get the money and return Aisha's sister.

However, Najah had recognized Anisa as the sister of her boyfriend, so if Anisa was to let her go, her days would have been numbered.

There was no other alternative than to kill her.

Her very own existence depended upon this.

As any other sane person would have done when faced with life, or death, she chose to live.

The weaving just wouldn't stop there.

She had noticed that Aisha had begun to grow fond of her.

In her attempts to exploit this obsession, Anisa allowed herself to get sucked in emotionally.

Before she knew it, she had been really feeling Aisha.

She hated the fact that Makeebah was who stopped the growth of their relationship.

Once the opportunity had presented itself to get rid of her, Anisa done so, or at least believes she was doing so.

Anisa never anticipated Aisha actually killing Makeebah.

In order to get rid of Makeebah, Anisa had to take matters into her own hands.

She had replaced the DNA sample that Aisha had given her with the samples of Makeebah.

Instead of Mujahid getting the rap for the death of whoever, Anisa created a situation.

She had believed she was killing two birds with one stone.

She had found the perfect opportunity when Aisha walked in on her phone call.

She had known that her partner she used to execute the kidnapping was getting hostile about the money.

Anisa had put the money up.

And was gone divide it after the heat cooled down.

Her partner had felt the time was then to get his cut.

Her efforts to calm him down were being diverted by his lack of patience.

He wanted to ball out of control, become something he wasn't.

Anisa knew it was only a matter of time before he went broke.

Rather than risk the chance of him putting the pressure down on her for her cut, she decided to eliminate him.

That way he couldn't hurt her in no way possible.

The thought of extortion, to exposing her hand for another piece of the pie, had entered her mind.

There was no way Anisa was gone let that happen.

Once Aisha walked in, it was her time to get her academy award.

She again persuaded Aisha into believing that her partner was in fact in cahoots with Kay in the kidnapping of her sister.

That was the perfect time to spill the DNA she had conjured up.

Aisha had believed she was setting up Mujahid, but was actually getting Makeebah out of the picture for Anisa's own benefit.

To Anisa, all that was okay, because the graces of Mujahid was her new focus.

Aisha had her chance to commit and ignored the advances of Anisa.

The betrayal issued by Aisha was justification for Anisa's endeavors.

Although, they had been in advancement of the situation at hand, they still were warranted according to Anisa's thought process.

The issue that baffled her the most was explaining to Mujahid that he was actually her last resort.

By Aisha not wanting to reciprocate the love given, caused Anisa to choose her second choice, it just so happened to be Mujahid.

She had wanted all the comforts of being with a man that she was entitled to. Not just any man, she had wanted Mujahid.

With her emotional connections to Aisha, the reality of that matter was virtually impossible.

Had circumstances been different there might have been an us, referring to the union of her and Mujahid, She thought to herself.

Anisa's infatuation caused her to do the ultimate of sins in the eyes of Aisha.

Anisa had took advantage of the opportunity forced upon her by Aisha.

Once Mujahid had managed to make his way into the heavens of her soul, she used that moment to get into the sanctuary of his world.

She had followed him throughout his ventures that morning he left her.

When the time was right, she seized the opportunity to rid Aisha of all distractions that would be in the way of their union.

Anisa took it upon herself to off Mujahid.

Now because the attempt was unsuccessful, she felt she had given herself a second chance to start over again.

She just needed a way to convey to Mujahid that she was a pawn in Aisha's game, forced to do the dirty deed without letting on that she had been involved with Aisha.

Forgiveness is what she needed.

Acceptance is what she wanted.

Both were actions that only Mujahid was capable of offering.

The likeliness of such a performance by Mujahid was slim to none.

How was it gone be possible for him not only to forgive, but accept into his life the woman responsible for his physical state.

It's because of her that he'll never walk again, never have the opportunity to experience the sweet nectars of a woman, never be able to be complete.

And most of all, never be able to populate the earth with the spawns of his loins.

Even though Mujahid had a son, he still wanted his little girl to complete his vision of the end result of life's treasures.

Pulling up and parking in the parking lot, Anisa grabs the steering wheel and begins to beat on it as if it had stolen something from her.

The rage exhibited was dangerous to conceive, yet alone, keep bottle up inside one's self.

The tears streaming down her face gave the impression she had been really remorseful for her actions.

Dreading the longest walk of her life, or at least it seemed to be at that moment, into the actual rehabilition center Mujahid had been in, Anisa exits her vehicle to do so.

After pondering the work she's actually done, Anisa came to the conclusion that it was easier to actually do the deeds than to come face to face with the after effects of her work.

Still confused and undecided as to how to pull this off, Anisa enters the room and greets Mujahid as a wife does her husband in his time of need.

All the support imaginable was so gallantly expressed.

Happy to see Anisa, Mujahid in a whispering voice says, "Hey babygirl."

For the whole time since his ordeal Anisa had been his rock.

She held him up when he was unable to do it himself.

She lifted his spirits when they were low enough to be on the negative side of the visibility scales.

She helped him to see that his self-worth was more than the spawns his loins could produce. But in fact, the impressions he's left on the impressionable lives he's touched and will continue to touch.

Anisa responds, "I'm a be alright now that I'm here with you." In a tone that symbolized pain and hurt from deep within her soul.

"That ain't sound too good... What's wrong miss lady?" He says in the same raspy whispers that his voice had already been in.

"I'm good... I just got a lot weighing on my heart.'She says.

"Just as you've been here for me... let me be there for you in your time of need." He says in a whisper that the sincerity could be heard.

Just as Anisa was about to answer, a nurse comes in and says in a happy go lucky pleasant tone, "Time for your bath and treatment horse..." Referring to the size of his member.

Anisa instantly caught an attitude and in a snotty sarcastic tone she spews out, "You can give him his treatment... I'm a give him his bath." Then lets out a sarcastic chuckle to imitate the goofier side of the nurse.

The nurse didn't bother to dignify the remark with a response.

Instead she surrendered the sponge over to Anisa to do as she said.

On the way out the nurse threw back an irking statement that irritated the fuck out of Anisa.

"Hit your button when she done... Horse."

Anisa rolled her eyes and went ahead and bathed Mujahid.

During the course of the bathing, Anisa sporadically dropped hints that no matter what he could always count on her for support.

Almost like she was trying to nurture him into nursing the idea of becoming dependent upon her.

Mujahid grabs her hand to stop the effects of his bathing and asks, "What's up?...

I'm a big boy, I don't cry! Say what's on your mind."

Staring her in the eyes so she could see the seriousness in his face. Then goes on to finish, "I always been a realistic dude, I can handle all aspects of life!

I'm not naive... I know shit happens, but your job as my boo is to keep shit funky at all times! Don't sugar coat shit!

Tell me what I'm supposed to know, as opposed to, what you think I wanna hear."

After hearing that, Anisa drops a tear and embraces Mujahid.

She then whispers into his ear, "That's why I love you!...

But it's some things that just ain't that easy to accept."

Now Mujahid is damn near begging to know what's going on.

After a few seconds of absorbing the jewel she had just dropped, Her remarks sparked all types of wheels in his head to begin to turn. As well as, a host of emotions running through his body.

The biggest being curiosity.

A few more seconds of holding him, Anisa lets go.

And stares into his eyes until Mujahid read, Forever Yours, in them.

Before he could speak to return the sentiments, Anisa breaks down and spills her soul.

At least the lesser of the evils.

She made Mujahid aware of her contact with Aisha.

She explained that Aisha was the one who encouraged her to come see him, but it was his conversation and personality that hooked her.

Anisa never let Aisha know that her and Mujahid were into each other and established a bond.

Nor did she drop the bomb on him by telling him she was the one who sat him down.

She first wanted to get a reaction from the bit she did allow to escape.

Mujahid had been taken aback.

He felt a certain type disgust for Anisa, as well as, betrayed.

Unable to speak, he just looked with a stare of death on his face.

Just as he was about to comment on the news, Anisa begins to spill more blood on the already stained surface.

Still not letting out that she was the shooter.

At this point Mujahid had put aside the lashing originally he was gone give her.

He decided to use the bitch instead.

She opened the doors for whatever.

And the shitty end of the stick she was gone get.

All that ran through his mind was getting back at Aisha for doing this to him.

If it meant eating shit for a bit, then so be it.

He was determined to kill Aisha.

Then at a later date deal with Anisa.

Right now, his focus is Aisha.

He asks, "So where you at with it now?"

Referring to her loyalty.

He could care less who her loyalty lied with, her true colors had been shown.

He was a firm believer that a leopard doesn't change spots.

If her disloyalty kicked in once, best believe it's gone seep out again somewhere down the line.

She was a waste of human life in his eyes.

"I'm wit you, always have been." She replies with all the comforts of being at his disposal.

"We gone let water flow beneath the bridge and move on...

Where Aisha at now?" He asks in a sinister type tone that gave the illusion that his raspy whispering voice was an act for an evil villain in a movie.

"Oh yeah... I was gone tell you that too..."

Before she could finish her statement Mujahid gave a look of Damn Bitch!... When do it stop!

"Aisha at my house tied up.

I didn't know what to do with her until you gave me the word to move." She continued.

Mujahid felt a tightness in his chest, almost like his heart was trying to jump out from the rapid beating it was doing.

Taking a minute to get his composure back in place, he instructs Anisa to get him out of the rehab immediately.

Scrambling to get his things together, Anisa is now leery to finish her confession.

It just might be a possibility that a new start is in the works.

Not able to find any clothing deemed appropriate to wear in public, Mujahid instructs Anisa, "Just put a pair of drawers on me... Some socks and a gown. Just get me out of here now."

Along the way to Anisa's place, Mujahid had her make a stop.

The taste of victory was overwhelming in the buds of his mouth.

He had been excited as well as repulsed.

He knew Aisha was already gone.

He just wanted her to see that her attempt to kill him was in vain.

She may have sat him down in a chair paralyzed from the waist down, but he was gone erase her existence from the world.

Then afterwards, Anisa had to bite the bullet.

There was no way possible for her to remain in play, and breathing the same air as him.

For now, she safe.

Once he fulfills his obligations to Aisha, best believe she gone be in a pine box right next to her.

For the remainder of the ride, Mujahid fantasized about the way he was gone kill both these bitches.

The idea was so appealing to him, that in his mind, he could feel his dick get hard.

At their first destination, Anisa pulls up to a condo out in Delaware County.

Mujahid tells her to go inside.

He figured it would be faster to have her grab his tools of engagements than to go through the hassle of getting him out the car and fumbling with his wheelchair.

He tells her, "Soon as you go in, go straight to the coffee table...

Underneath it, you gone have to move it.

And pull the rug back.

Grab the black briefcase out of the safe."

Then he gave her a combination to a safe that had been in the floor, hidden in a perfect spot.

Once Anisa got in, she was astounded at how beautiful the structure and interior was.

This place was a page straight out of Better Homes and Gardens.

Italian leather furniture, glass tables trimmed in 24 karat gold. Marble floors that had been engraved with his initials at the point of entry, so that whoever crossed his threshold knew where they were at.

There was no mistaking who shit you was in.

The appearance alone demanded appreciation as well as respect.

After taking in the vision of what beauty truly was, Anisa gets to the task given to her.

Just as he said, she followed his instructions to the letter.

And just as he said, it would be a safe.

She opens it.

Once opened, she couldn't help but to notice how neat and organized it had been.

There weren't the expectants of what a safe should have in it.

Instead she found briefcases. All lined up with numbers on them.

And on the end was a single black one.

It really stood out since the others was brown.

They each had combination locks on them.

Curious to know what was in them, but not wanting to betray Mujahid's trust, Anisa grabs what she was supposed to and fixes everything back as she found it.

Taking one last look at how elegant and pretty this place had been before leaving.

In her mind, she had been in the home of her dreams.

Now back at the car, she slides the briefcase through the passenger side window and head around the car to get into the driver's seat.

By the time she gets in, Mujahid already had the case open.

it was a gun that looked fake.

Not real, or at least not like nothing she had ever seen before.

Along the side of the box of bullets inside read, .454 Raging Bull.

As Mujahid loaded it, she noticed it only took four shots.

However, the bullets had to have been at least three inches long.

And as thick around as a broomstick.

There wasn't no doubt that if somebody got hit by that gun, they would be dismantled instantly.

She dreaded to think of what was next to come for Aisha.

Then began her journey to unite Mujahid and Aisha one last time.

38 DEADLY REUNION, NEW BEGINNING

For the duration of the ride to her apartment, Anisa listened to the words that found their way out of Mujahid's mouth.

The tone... The vibe... The allure of his speech was anything but forgiving.

She had been in this predicament time and time again, each time the same outcome.

In fact, one could say she was kind of insane.

She believed that by doing the same things that landed her at this point over and over again was acceptable. And somehow, eventually the results would change.

Despite her method of thought, one thing she was sure of was that the gleam in Mujahid's eyes didn't read acceptance.

She read trickery, deceit, usury and ultimately vengeance.

The more he spoke the more she felt her back was pinned to the wall.

She couldn't chance allowing her feelings to be brought to light.

She just allowed him to speak.

And by doing so, it allowed her time to think of how to get herself out of this situation.

Meanwhile, Mujahid had been rambling on, not sounding convincing at all.

The words he spoke sounding as hollow as the emptiness of a milk carton.

The gestures he used were as limp and lifeless as a soggy spaghetti noddle.

The look in his eyes let the cat out the bag, that revenge had no boundaries or limitations.

His soul had been incapable of offering forgiveness.

Not trying to let on to how he felt, his cold stares only mimicked the sentiments of, you next bitch!

Anisa felt the animosity that he tried to shovel under the piles of shit.

There was no way on God's green earth she was gone allow herself to become a victim once again.

Under no circumstances was that gone happen.

The wheels in her head began to turn in warp speed.

All her life, Anisa always been the type woman who couldn't handle rejection.

For those that done so to her, always seemed to face sudden fatalities.

This wasn't gone be no different.

In her last situation Kay felt she was smothering him. He just needed time to be apart to gather his thoughts.

Anisa didn't see it that simple.

In her head he been trying to abandon her.

Its because of that line of thinking that's leading her to the place she at dealing with Mujahid and Aisha.

Jail ain't never been in her forecast, so she used the cut throat ruthlessness of Aisha to get rid of Kay.

However, rather than rid her of her troubles, it only created more problems.

Now once again she's faced with the creative thinking and planning necessary to come out of this shit unscathed and paid.

Before they got to Anisa's apartment, she asks, "Once you come face to face with your desire, then what?" Just to spark a reaction.

"What you mean, then what?" He shouted back with expressions and emotions to be read as, where the fuck you going with this bitch!

Breaking his brief moment of silence to continue with, "I'm gone kill this bitch!

Does that answer your question?"

"Actually it doesn't." She says in response to his question.

"I was talking about us...

Where do we go from there?

Is it even gone be an us?

I ain't no angel by far...

I've made mistakes along the way..."

All that ran through her mind while she was speaking was, not killing you was the biggest.

"But still...

I'm here ready to commit...

Ready to be the woman you not only want...

The one you need, but most of all, the one you Deserve."

In his mind, her little speech had been appealing.

Her words touched his heart, but nevertheless, her fate was etched in stone.

All he could think to come back with was, "We'll see."

That response alone, set in concrete what Anisa had to do.

There was no second guessing.

By the time they had arrived at her apartment, she was already in motion doing what was needed to see better days.

When they entered the apartment, all the fury, rage and anticipation that once overtook Mujahid had been reduced to hesitation and procrastination.

He had known what he came to do, but seeing Aisha laying there so lifeless struck a chord in his heart.

To visualize the death of a loved one was one thing.

To actually see it, was a whole other world.

All the emotions that captivated him in the beginning had suddenly come back to revamp the love he had still harbored deep down within his soul.

Looking at her, he could only offer his tears as consultation to console his emotions.

He had seemed to enter a realm that he didn't want to visit.

Lost in space, drifting to a once better place, he reminisced about the cherishable moments they had shared in their stolen moments together.

He seen everything from the long walks in the breezes of the night air for ice cream.

To the tender moments exploring passion only felt in the presence of one another.

He envisioned the not so great moments.

When the world seemed to be extremely cold, and turned its back on him, it was Aisha that offered her arms as warmth, and her bossoms as a resting place.

The arguments that seemed so major at the time, now seemed to be frivolous.

Although he had been sitting in a chair now, his memories somehow instantly placed an occupied sign in a section of his heart where forgiveness resided.

Yet, somehow that small section couldn't superseded the areas where hatred had taken residence.

Being brought back by the echoes of Anisa's voice, Mujahid asks,

"Is she dead?"

"No... She just sleeping. She'll be up in a minute."

"What happened to her? Why does she appear to be so worn?"

"She was shot by Makeebah." Anisa responds.

"When all this took place?" He asked.

"A couple days ago."

"Why you ain't say nothing to me?" He asked in an irritated tone.

"I was in a battle within myself...

You won...

That's why we here now."

Seeing movement from Aisha brought the conversation to a halt.

Mujahid rolled around the bed so that his face was the first one she seen when her eyes opened.

Once the movement stopped, and slumber had taken its place again, Mujahid got impatient.

He began to splash water into her face to induce her waking up.

After a few splashes, Aisha awakens and goes into a frenzy.

Just as he wanted, his face was what she saw first.

And death was second.

The once all too pleasant glares from his chinky eyes had been replaced with emptiness and darkness of his soul.

Just like the visuals that had been drafted by society of what the grim reaper should look like.

Aisha pulled herself together and accepted the fate that was about to surface.

Then looks over to Anisa and says, "Bitch you was playing me the whole time!...

I'm a deal with you in hell, soon as you get there!"

Anisa payed her no mind.

Instead she lowered her gaze to the heights of the floor and exited the room.

Mujahid then asked, "Of all people... Why you?" Trying to find closure to the acts of betrayal that she exhibited.

"What you mean...

Nigga you ain't no saint!

I was a target for your scopes to hit, so I tried to beat you to the punch." She says in a hostile tone that said she had no regrets, or remorse for her actions.

"I was hurt by your actions, but killing you wasn't an option...

You were my wife.

I took a vow to protect, love and cherish your ungrateful rotten ass."

"So it's gone end like this? At least untie me so I can stand on my feet." She said trying to remain within the codes of the street.

"Bitch this was all a game to you?" He asks in a tone that illustrated his pain to the fullest.

Then goes on to continue with, "G's die on their feet...

Dick eating lizards die on their backs."

Then the screams of a mega sized cannon went off.

And before she knew it, it was all over.

One thing that can be said is, she ain't suffer.

It had been instant upon impact.

Anisa heard the screams of the cannon.

Then opened the bedroom door to see what exactly had went down.

What she seen was something out of a horror show.

Mujahid had been sitting there drenched in the splatters of her blood.

Still holding his gun.

And silently crying with the rivers of tears overlapping the matter that had been stuck to his face.

Aisha had been in pieces, literally.

That one shot had seemed to sever her head from her torso.

And sections of her chest had holes in it.

Blood had engulfed the paint of the room.

The bed frame she had been lying on had somehow broke and fell to the floor.

The mere sight of the damage Mujahid's gun had done left Anisa in terror like she never experienced in her life.

Thinking she was next, she rushes over to Mujahid.

Standing behind him just in case he wanted to let another shot loose before her surprise had arrived.

Her focus was to keep him calm and relaxed.

Just allow him to absorb the moment he had been in.

But at the same time, keep him from entering a zone that would warrant her actions being dealt with.

She embraces and holds on to him for dear life.

What Mujahid didn't know was, that in a fraction of a minute, he was on his way to the penitentiary to serve the remainder of his days.

That would be the deal.

If he elected to go to trial, then a needle would certainly seal his fate.

Anisa had dialed 911 prior to leaving the room.

Then dropped her phone on the floor.

It wasn't that Aisha's words had struck a note in her conscious that caused her to wallow in self-pity, she was just making sure the call went through to the police.

The whole conversation was being recorded.

When she left out she fabricated a story that would land her in the innocent column.

Without Aisha there to speak, who could attest to the fact she was involved.

At the very moment Mujahid had come out his sulk, the police were there, guns drawn and ready to shoot.

He heard one of the officers tell him to, "Drop his weapon."

It was at that moment the consequences of his actions had actually hit him.

He begins to see himself wither away without nothing to look forward to but commissary.

The ideal of sitting in somebody's box awaiting to become antique furnishings was a vision he'd rather do without.

He had always looked at those type of dudes in the penitentiary as idiots.

They would rather be depressed and tolerant of the inhumane behavior that they had been sentenced to for the rest of their days, as opposed to standing firm on their actions and deciding their own fate.

The life he had was gone.

He had lived to the fullest of his potential.

He found love.

Had the experience of being in love.

He had traveled the globe.

Seen and done in his short time, what many spend an eternity trying to see and do.

He fucked and sucked some of the baddest bitches to walk the planet.

As well as, experienced the vast majority of nationalities in the world.

He came.

He saw.

He conquered.

He was at the end of the road.

With his accomplishments outweighing his future endeavors, he made the decision to go out as a soldier.

He raised his gun in a manner that one would have thought had been adjusted to slow motion, while simultaneously seeing any hope of coming out of this incident alive, being shattered.

Rock out with your cock out was the last words he would ever speak.

Before he could get a chance to even fathom letting a shot off, the officers had his body dancing in his chair.

Anisa turns and sees his bullet ridden carcass lying slumped over in his wheelchair, bleeding from every orifice possible.

His mouth agape with fragments of his tongue being missing.

She had under estimated the actions of Mujahid.

Never did she entertain the end playing out as it did.

The most she gave him was having an altercation before apprehension.

His actions only fed and confirmed her speculations that prison wasn't a place she wanted to be.

EPILOGUE

A few months later, the investigation had come to a close.

Anisa made her way to the P.N.C National Bank located in Center City.

She withdrawals a key from a safety security box she had been occupying.

Then proceeded to the Philadelphia National Airport.

Along the way, the events that lead up to this point in her life, all seem to flash before her eyes.

There was no grief involved behind the lives that had been taken.

Nor was it any remorse for the families who lost loved ones.

However, there was gratitude extended to the not so willing participants that helped to make her vision a reality.

The only sentiments she was capable of processing was that she had been stupid for only getting a mill out of the deal. As opposed to the maximum she could have received.

The one thing she never wanted to become had in fact transpired.

The only comforts of being a baby's mama, was the money she was in route to retrieve.

Out of the clear blue she breaks out into a hysterical chuckle, explaining to the unborn fetus she had been carrying that, "Your daddy made sure you were well taken care of...

You not gone want for nothing.

Mama is now big mama!

All you have to do is get here healthy."

Once she reaches the airport, she gets the duffle bag out of the locker she had reserved.

She exits in a hurry to begin building the life that she's always wanted for herself and her child.

On her way out, she bumped into a young fella.

"Oh... I'm sorry sir." She says offering apologies for running into him.

"It's cool ma... If I had to be touched by somebody, I'm just glad it was an angel." The man offers back with a smile that caught her attention.

Extending his hand for a light hand shake he also adds, "I'm Khalil."

"I'm Anisa." She says back in an innocent toned voice.

"Let me help you with that?" He says reaching for her bag.

"No it's cool... I got it."

"At least let me feed you... You in that much of a hurry you can't eat?" He asks in a sincere, yet, pleasant tone that showed interest in her.

After contemplating for a brief moment, she agreed to have lunch with Khalil.

After all, she was in a position to fulfill all her fantasies and dreams.

The only thing missing was a man to love and love her back.

They entered one of the restaurants that was there at the airport's terminal to eat and to get to know one another.

"A toast." Khalil says while lifting his glass of water.

Anisa found that gesture to be in good humor. As well as, cute.

Then Khalil goes on to continue, "To better standings and a new leash on life."

"I'll drink to that." Anisa offers smiling as to show interest in Khalil and his sentiments.

They sat there chatting for a spell before realizing that they had both ran with the same circle of associates and never came across one another.

Khalil was in fact the young boy that lead Kay to Aisha.

Anisa didn't know that.

She had just been familiar with his knowledge of Aisha.

Before long, they became on item.

Anisa helped him to get to the level he only dreamed of in his life.

She had the baby.

He was on board to raise the lil' girl.

Especially, since he had believed it was his child.

Life finally played out in a manner Anisa felt she deserved.

The only thing missing was a ring on her finger and the changing of her last name.

Other than that, she was in heaven with the life she was exploring.

She was never a firm believer of Karma.

And she was within her means not to, considering the beautiful life she had, despite the evilness of her soul.